DYANDI

Timothy Doyle

M

MELBOURNE BOOKS

Published by Melbourne Books
Level 9, 100 Collins Street,
Melbourne, VIC 3000
Australia
www.melbournebooks.com.au
info@melbournebooks.com.au

National Library of Australia
Cataloguing-in-Publication entry
Author: Doyle, Timothy.
Title: Dyandi / Professor Timothy Doyle.
ISBN: 9781922129376 (paperback)
Subjects: Environmentalism--Fiction.
Environmental policy--Fiction.
Dewey Number: A823.4

To my sister Jenny,

my brothers Greg and Malachi,

and the B'laan people of Mindanao —

all noble compatriots and fierce survivors.

Acknowledgements

So many people need to be acknowledged in the researching, writing, editing and publication phases of this book. To the peoples of Mindanao and Central Australia (most of whom must remain nameless for obvious reasons): your daily struggles for survival against vast transnational extractive companies, against seemingly impossible odds, have provided the inspiration and the life lessons that have forced my hand to write this book.

To the activists who have travelled through similar environmental campaigns and journeys with me over the years — thanks for the friendship, the passion and the commitment. Particular acknowledgement must go to Len Webb, Don Henry, Phil Tighe, Ros Taplin, Peter Hay, Geoff Mosley, Michelle Grady, Sarah Wright, Avel Sichon and Cam Walker.

Next, I'd like to express my indebtedness to my students of both environmental politics and political fiction. These brave souls generously followed my instructions by enthusiastically crossing the imagined (but all-too-powerful) non-fictional/fictional divide on an everyday basis, allowing me to introduce storytelling as a means of uniting and exploring the public and private political realms. This unquestioned but artificial divide in the study, writing and celebration of politics will one day, hopefully, be a thing of the past.

Next, enormous gratitude must be registered to the staff and students of the creative writing postgraduate program at the University of Adelaide; in particular, Jan Harrow, Phil Edmonds and Nick Jose.

To my editors at different times of the writing project. I could not be more appreciative for the wisdom and craft of Jan Harrow, Patrick Allington, Katia Ariel and, finally, Chloe Brien of Melbourne Books. Thanks also to my sister, Jenny Goldsmith, and to my daughter, Georgia Lawrence-Doyle, for thorough readings of the work in its earlier stages.

Credit must be given to both Lucille and Anna Gore. To Anna, the beautiful painting on the front cover is tribute to your enormous skill as an artist. To Lucille, I am most grateful for the valuable administrative assistance that allowed me to ultimately place this work.

I must express particular gratitude to David Tenenbaum of Melbourne Books, who has the temerity, courage and imagination to continue to publish books such as mine during a period when independent publishing in Australia is under such enormous market pressures.

To my parents, Maureen and Seamus, thanks for instilling in me both the beauty and importance of the written word.

And finally, I'd like to record my deepest and most heartfelt thanks to Fiona Lawrence, my partner, for always believing in this project and insisting that I persevere with it.

Tim Doyle
February 2014

Contents

Prologue

The knife was sharp. He opened his hand painlessly, gladly. Blood spilled into the bowl, heavy droplets falling into the crimson mass. The vessel was passed around with the motion of the sun, from dusk 'til dawn, each warrior adding his life to the whole. At last it came to rest at the feet of the chief.

The chant began: a high pitch of staccato rhythms blended with pungent smoke, the forest's earthiness and the fecund darkness of night. Sparks burst, illuminating the men's wide-eyed faces, their vulnerabilities rather than their strengths captured in this brief display of frenzied light.

When silence fell, the chief took the bowl to his lips and drank from it. Tom realised the fullness of what they now expected of him. This isn't the blood of Christ, *he thought*, this isn't wine. It is the very essence of the B'laan people.

When the bowl came to him once more, he fought the desire to gag. He tried to blank it out, like a child does when taking foul medicine, and concentrated instead on the ritual's importance. Solidarity is the power of the powerless, *he thought.* He was not alone, after all.

He moved the cup to his lips. Tiny worm-like insects wriggled in the thick liquor. Maggots or parasites? *he wondered.* Too late now. And what did it really matter? When his tongue first tasted the sweet-salty warmth of the mixture his gut lurched. Lowering the bowl in front of him, saliva gushed into his mouth — the precursor to vomit. Fighting hard against the reflex, he did not dare look up at the warriors' faces. He summoned his strength of purpose and, in a sheer act of will, raised the bowl once more, taking a deep draught of the bloody soup.*

1

The Portal

Tom hated seeing his name on a piece of cardboard at airports. He wanted to slip quietly into the country, get his bearings and settle in. He wanted to take a shower, maybe shuffle down to the hotel bar before having a meal, ring home to tell Amanda he'd arrived safely, and then hit the hay nice and early. He moved at pace, 'in the right lane' as he commonly called it, passing all who walked in the same direction. Even when standing still, he led with his chin, his tall body tilted forward.

But despite his wishes, as he left customs and walked into the gunpowder smells and shrieking noises of the humid Manila night, a smiling, finely-built Filipino man looked straight at him, holding the dreaded card with his name on it: Dr Thomas McMahon. Tom's first inclination was to ignore it, bolt and hail a taxi, but before he could plan an escape the man had grabbed his hand luggage, urging Tom to follow.

The man laughed with delight. 'I'm Paul ... Paul Benguet. Welcome to the Philippines!' he said in an American accent. 'Any more bags?'

Tom shook his head, venturing an ice-breaker with, 'You're the Paul from the emails?'

'You got it. Well c'mon then, let's go ... we've been waiting for you.' He put his head down and pushed through the throng.

While Tom was dressed for the heat in light cotton trousers and a short-sleeved check shirt, the tweed coat over his arm advertised that he was an alien from the much cooler world of Melbourne winter. He had already broken out in a sweat, the skin on his forearms itching in protest to the prickly fabric draped across it. He only carried two bags: his brown leather satchel for his books and papers, and an overnight bag for his clothes. He always travelled light, so he kicked himself for bringing the tweed jacket.

He looked at Paul a little enviously. In his t-shirt splashed with bright reds and yellows, and his comfortable jeans, he didn't look like a human rights lawyer. Weaving his way through the crowd, Tom kept his eyes on Paul's frizzy ponytail.

'You want a taxi?' people kept yelling at them.

'You want a room? Big, beautiful room. Bath?'

'You want to buy package tour to beautiful beach?'

'You want artefact?'

Eventually, they reached a compact woman thrumming her hands on the bonnet of a rusted-out minibus. She wore a sleeveless camera jacket and her thick black hair was stuffed up under a wide-brimmed peaked cap. She jumped quickly from the front of the van to the rear, agitation quivering through her body. Nodding at Paul, she locked her massive, dark brown eyes on Tom.

'So, you must be Dr McMahon. Maria Cortes,' she began, also in perfect American English.

She shook his hand briefly and firmly, the strength of the grip belying her size. Her sternness couldn't mask the fact that she was a beautiful woman, and this gave Tom an unexpected feeling of unease.

'Ms Cortes,' he replied.

She looked at him as if he were already a nuisance. 'Your schedule has been arranged. Please gather your luggage and put it in the back of the van. We're going directly to the compound. Thank you.'

Compound, he thought. *What the hell's that supposed to mean?*

'Maria, perhaps you didn't get my email, but I'm already booked to stay at the Seafarer's and I—'

'Yes, yes, we got your email. But there is no time for the hotel.'

And that was the end of that. Maria took the wheel. She insisted Paul sit next to her and now they chatted in their own language, hardly stopping for breath. Tom sat hunched in the back, his legs too long for the space provided. He knew he would have to *perform* later on, without a shower or rest, to muster his people skills and attempt to be charming. He turned his torso away from the others, imagining himself as an island, and stared out the window.

The fatigue washed through him, as if some vital plug had been removed from his core, his listlessness in stark contrast to what was outside his window. There were no lines on the roads, no columns of traffic, no passing lanes. People travelled in and on the tops of cars, jeeps, buses and trucks. Some rode bicycles, others horses and donkeys. Many walked. On the back of one truck, a man's legs and torso dangled in mid-air. He linked his arms through the arms of two other men to stop from dropping onto the road.

It was stifling in the van with the windows closed, but when he opened the small vent window, a thick, hot, lead-based soup of car exhaust and dust hit him. The air left an acidic tang at the base of his tongue. He closed the window and noticed that many of the people on the open-windowed buses or walking at the side of the road held handkerchiefs to their mouths.

On top of this, Maria and Paul smoked heavily. Tom's sinuses constricted. He leaned over the partition. 'Look, I'm not a smoker myself. Would you mind ...?' he said, pointing to Maria's cigarette.

Maria wound her window down and threw the finished cigarette onto the road. She then snapped her fingers at Paul. Tom looked at the packet as Paul handed it to her. *No unleaded fuel or low-tar cigarettes here*, he thought. Maria lit up and inhaled deeply.

'Your first lesson in the Philippines, Dr McMahon,' Maria said.

'You see, we have more likely ways of dying here than simply smoking cigarettes.'

When they stopped for gasoline Paul forced open the sliding door on the side of the rusted van. 'Dr McMahon, you jump in the front. Maria wants to brief you on a couple of things. There have been some fairly big developments.'

'Like what?'

'Maria will fill you in,' he said, turning away to refuel the car. Paul performed a series of gliding motions; one moment he existed in one place, the next in another.

When they set off again, Tom sat sandwiched uncomfortably between his two companions. Maria lit another cigarette from the one she was finishing and turned the radio up for a Whitney Houston song that didn't sound much like Whitney Houston.

'Filipinos love music, Dr McMahon,' she said.

'Please, call me Tom.'

She hummed along to the tune for a while, then asked, 'How long have you known Jack Collins?'

'Since we were children.'

'A fine journalist.' She swung the wheel heavily, avoiding another car. Tom's heart pounded but Maria Cortes appeared to have barely noticed the potential calamity. 'You've been to the Philippines before?'

'No, this is my first time.'

She rolled her window down and flicked ash impatiently, sighed and then sang a couple more bars, her eyes darting over the road in front of her.

'Dr McMahon. I don't know how much Jack Collins has told you, but the timing of your visit is quite good. I've managed to get you onto an International Fact-Finding Mission for the National People's Organisation.'

'Jack hasn't told me anything.'

'Good. ... You know of the NPO?'

'No.'

She exhaled emphatically. 'They are the major people's organisation in the Philippines. The NPO is a broad coalition of human rights, labour and environmental organisations. We're going to an NPO compound now. You'll be told more about the IFFM, the Mission, then.'

'Mission?'

'Yes — like I just told you — the International Fact-Finding Mission. You'll be part of a team investigating the Horizon Mining Corporation's operations in Mindanao. That's what you've come for, isn't it?'

'Yes ... though I had no idea I was to be part of an organised group. I just thought I'd go down to Mindanao and meet up with some of—'

'Dr McMahon,' said Maria, her eyes ablaze, nostrils flaring with smoke. She tossed her hair back from her face. 'Two points you must understand. One: no-one *just goes down to Mindanao*. And two: we are busy people. We have inquisitive foreigners coming here all the time. Few offer us anything useful. We have worked out the best way you can contribute. Forgive me if I sound somewhat rude, but we have no room for passengers here.'

The words 'inquisitive foreigners' stung him. Didn't she know he might have some information to share from the Australian campaign against HMC? He bit his tongue, wondering how it was that no-one had told her how much he could contribute — how much relevant information about HMC he actually had. Alright, he acknowledged that he was just a volunteer. But his organisation had elected him President and, more often than not, he possessed more real power than the professional bureaucrats who ran the Environment Centre on an everyday basis. It was he who was the official spokesperson, and it was his head which sat firmly on the legal chopping block in their own dealings with HMC.

He would have liked to still be in the back of the van, in his own world, or even wedged up against the passenger window. Instead, he had to look ahead into the upcoming maelstrom of traffic, with Maria Cortes hitting him with the gear stick every time she changed down, making him conscious of what were, in the Philippines, his overly long legs. *No room for passengers*, he thought.

They were off the main airport highway now, moving at walking pace through narrow, heavily congested streets. There were no concrete footpaths, though there did seem to be areas belonging more to pedestrians than cars. Cooking smells — hot oils, deep fried food, unknown spices tickling high up on the inside of his nose — blended with the sickening pungency of burning fuel, probably kerosene. The stench of human faeces and urine rose from the gutters and grabbed his throat. The humidity, coupled with the pollution, meant that the smell could not escape into the atmosphere, but hung under a damp blanket of smog so thick that Tom felt as if he could rub its oily dankness between thumb and forefinger.

His nausea was made worse by the saturated colours everywhere, from the stuttering kaleidoscope of people's clothing to the gaudiness of the foodstuffs in the market stalls. There were no packages of shapeless frozen meats here. Instead heads, still-beating hearts and innards of chickens, ducks, goats and pigs hung from butchers' hooks in brightly lit windows. The moment of their earthly exit had been captured in a myriad of death masks, tongues falling bloated from their mouths.

It seemed to Tom that every third man toted a machine gun. They were standing next to automated teller machines, watching over every residential or commercial entrance. He felt surrounded by death, both real and imminent, human and non-human. He identified some of the gun-bearers as police — neatly pressed blue uniforms, sunglasses and moustaches — and others as military. Still, many others bore weapons without wearing any readily identifiable uniform.

The van's progress was now almost imperceptible. They spent more time stationary than in motion. Any time they stopped, populations of small children — holding smaller, often naked siblings in their arms — mobbed the van. Maria and Paul shushed them away without making eye contact.

Maria noticed Tom looking at the children. 'Don't gawk at them. If you do, they'll never go away.'

One boy launched himself onto the van's bonnet, an infant on each hip, and landed hard. As the babies howled, the boy — his eyes huge, his mouth ajar — held out his shaking hand. Tom looked away, his stomach aching.

After an hour of travelling through crowded city streets they arrived at their destination. It was now early evening. A guard stood in front of two immense steel gates, the only visible break in fifteen-foot high stone walls topped with razor wire. Tom had noticed that these fortifications were not unusual. Most houses in this area were surrounded by such walls.

Maria spoke to the guard who, in turn, leaned into the van through the driver's window and casually inspected Tom and Paul. When Maria showed the guard some papers, he jumped back to attention and gave the order to another guard inside the compound to open the gates.

Within the compound, two-storey buildings formed three parts of a quadrangle. The lawn in the middle surrounded a grotto arrangement comprising a large cross and some boulders. As they got their luggage out of the boot, Tom noticed crucifixes pinned to every available surface. He sensed a stillness hanging over him, a sensation that he shouldn't speak or make undue noise.

Paul ushered them along a veranda that ran down one side of the lawn. Tom felt self-conscious that his shoes squeaked on the slate floor. He glanced down at his feet. He always wore brown shoes. It hadn't been a conscious decision, at first. It was years later, in fact, that he understood why. Brown shoes meant that a man didn't care for fashion, didn't care unduly for the opinions of others.

At the end of the veranda, around the back of the building, was a larger meeting space — open to the air but with a low gazebo stretching overhead. A blackboard stood on an easel in the centre of the space, a sight Tom had not seen since childhood.

Paul gestured to him to put his bags down. 'Take a seat, thank you, Dr McMahon.'

They sat on plastic-backed chairs and waited. No explanation seemed forthcoming as to their purpose or agenda. Tom felt shattered from jet lag and sensory overload. He wanted to stow his gear away and chew the cud of the day. But he kept quiet.

Sitting surrounded by frangipanis in the humid dusk of a distant land, however lovely, he found himself without any roadmap or guiding principles, and this forced sensation of being on holiday was very challenging for him. He'd never 'gone with the flow' in all his life. *He* was the one who usually set timeframes for completion and operational agendas. *He* made things happen. Whether it was exhaustion or the instinct that he would not survive without some surrender, he decided then and there that he would try to behave differently here. He would take on the pace of life and its purpose when and where it presented itself to him. He inhaled the garden scents, sighed and his shoulders dropped.

Some minutes later, Maria emerged from inside the building with a young nun dressed in a full habit, despite the heat, and a stocky Filipino man who Tom thought was probably in his early forties. When the nun sat down in front of him, Tom shuffled his chair over to her.

'Hi,' he said quietly, extending his hand. 'I'm Tom McMahon ... from the Melbourne Environment Centre.'

Maria introduced the woman as Sister Borgias from the Catholic Freedom and Liberation Desk, based at the Catholic Community Hostel. The woman smiled but didn't speak. Then Maria introduced the man by his first name only: Enrico.

'He is the secretary-general of the National People's Organisation — the NPO. We are privileged to have the honour of his company,' Maria said, her face solemn.

There seemed a tightness about Enrico, his clean-shaven jaw clenched. He wore a white business shirt that showed ropes of muscle on the sides of his neck. But he quickly put Tom at ease, showing him a warm smile of bright white teeth and sandwiching both Tom's hands between his own.

'On behalf of the NPO, I wish to offer you — Dr McMahon — a warm welcome to the Philippines Republic. The people are happy you are here.'

Which people? Tom mused to himself.

'I suppose I had better explain our International Fact-Finding Missions. Forgive me if I do all the talking for a while. I'll take questions at the end.' Enrico paused, as if bracing himself for an uphill climb. His English — with an American twang — seemed textbook perfect, almost formal, as if educated abroad at one of the better universities as a diplomat or foreign affairs attaché.

'We find IFFMs a useful vehicle to investigate practices of transnational corporations and to focus our resistance,' Enrico began. 'Your presence in the Philippines opens doors for us. Many acts of repression against the people of the Philippines go on every day, with little scrutiny. But you ... as an international ... bring us more political mileage. You are worth more than we are, in the global scheme of things. We wish to write a report — with your help, of course — on our investigations to send to the United Nations. With you along, this will carry more weight.'

No-one had mentioned a report, Tom thought.

'The local media knows you are here and already has the spotlight on you. You are a very distinguished person, Dr McMahon ... and I know that your behaviour is beyond reproach, but from this point on you must imagine that your life is an open book. Please be very careful as to what you do and what you say. Only speak to the media after the NPO has approved your statements.'

Enrico turned to his left and nodded. 'Both Maria and Paul will accompany you to Mindanao. Maria Cortes will be your media liaison. Paul will handle our legal affairs there. You will be placed in the hands of Father Joseph Ricardo from the People's Environmental Alliance. They will form the local contingent of the Mission.'

Maria offered Enrico a cigarette and lit it for him. He inhaled sharply and then continued.

'A little about the Philippines and the NPO.' He moved to the blackboard, took up a bit of chalk and started writing numbers up on the slate. 'The Philippines are ruled by a small but extremely powerful elite of about one to two percent of the population in close collusion with northern imperialist interests.'

Tom winced; 'imperialism' was a term that grated on him. He hadn't heard it used since studying politics back at university in the eighties.

'This elite,' Enrico said, 'is closely aligned to the military. You will remember the coup that overthrew Marcos?'

Tom nodded.

'Although Marcos is now gone, the powerbrokers within the military remain in control. Aquino only came to power on the back of this military clique and the intervention of the CIA. It had less to do with 'People Power' as was reported … or with Imelda Marcos's shoes.'

Thank Christ he's got a sense of humour, thought Tom.

Enrico's face then turned grim, his toothy smile disappearing, his mouth pinched downwards. At the base of his nose, broken blood vessels swelled, their high colour flooding across his broad cheeks.

'The NPO supported Aquino in her struggle,' he said. 'After her ascendancy to power, for our efforts forty-five key members of the NPO vanguard, including my predecessor, were gunned down in front of our offices in downtown Manila. That is why we are here this evening, relying on the good grace of our comrades in the Catholic Church.'

'Vanguard', 'comrades': these were other words Tom thought had passed their use-by date. He wondered if Enrico knew that he represented an organisation concerned primarily with words like 'ecosystems', 'climate change' and 'biodiversity'. His Environment Centre opposed the HMC, but they hardly lobbied for revolution. Tom imagined what the professionals in his organisation would make of this; what his politically pragmatic CEO, Louise Roberts, would think if she was here. But again, an internal voice told him to be quiet for now.

'Since that time, we have not been involved in parliamentary democracy. Change can only come from the people.' Enrico moved to the blackboard again and scribbled some more numbers. 'Seventy-five percent of Filipinos are peasants living subsistence lifestyles. The rest are workers in towns and cities … and then, there is a small middle class. All these groups are the people NPO represents.'

'I know this may come as a bit of a shock for you,' Enrico continued. 'You come from a country where capitalism has such a hold that you think it is not an ideology at all, but just the way things are. But in the Philippines, capitalism hasn't won yet. Here, we have a battle between two major ideologies. We are in the midst of an historic struggle.'

He's sounding more like Mao every minute, Tom thought.

'By your affiliation with NPO your life is at risk, and this risk will increase sharply when you arrive in Mindanao. Do not go out in public by yourself. Do not attend cinemas, markets or bars where you can be targeted anonymously. You must understand, Dr McMahon, that we have powerful enemies. Many of us risk our lives every day in pursuit of our liberation. And you inherit our enemies. But also, you are in a double bind. Though you are here to help us, you also look like our oppressors. Many Filipinos, my people, will resent you for being here.'

Tom looked at Paul anxiously. But Paul just hunched his shoulders and gestured with open hands.

A gentle smile crept over Enrico's face. 'I don't mean to scare you, just to express concern for your safety. These things may not happen, but we all must be prepared for the worst. We are confronting powerful interests here.' He paused again. 'Tomorrow some of us will have business to attend to in Manila. The day after, you will leave for General Santos City in Mindanao. Once there, as I said, you will be entirely under the wing of Father Joseph Ricardo who, I'm sure, you have already heard of ... but enough for now. You must be tired and hungry. Goodnight.'

He clapped his hands and a number of men appeared from behind a stairwell. One moved to grab Tom's bag, gesturing with his head to follow him, while another escorted Paul. Tom looked back and saw Maria and the nun leave.

The man with Tom's bag took him up the flight of wooden stairs and then down another long corridor into the interior of the first storey of the building. Pictures of particularly bloody Christs and benign Holy Mothers, heads tilted downwards, hung the length of the passageway. The floors were covered in faded and worn green linoleum and the white walls were made of the type of perforated wood Tom had used to mount his tools on, back in his shed at home. The man pointed to the bathroom and then showed him to his room. He flung the door open, leaving without a word.

The room was more like a cell, no more than two square metres. Tom took in a wooden single bed covered in a faded yellow chenille bedspread. Frayed at the edges, the sheets were also worn but looked clean and crisp. The only other furniture in the room was a small bedside table. Above the bed hung another crucifix.

Throwing his stuff on the floor, Tom slid his shoes off and lay down. When he eventually managed to lie on his back, after stuffing his coat into the crevice in the middle of the bed, he noticed there was no ceiling in the cell. It was open to a much higher tin roof, and from the roof hung fans with light globes on their undersides. He worked out that one fan light serviced about half a dozen cells.

Despite the lack of a ceiling, it was stifling. Beads of moisture ran down the particle board walls and gathered in small pools on the linoleum floor. Any wind from the fan was only enough to wobble these droplets like tiny jellies.

As he tried to settle, there was a single knock at the door. By the time he got up and grabbed the door handle, there was no-one there — just an enamel plate of stew at his feet and a plastic cup of very weak lemon cordial. He realised, then, that he was starving. He ate the rice and non-descript stew quickly. It looked like it may have had chicken in it, but the bones were very small.

When he was done, he stripped off to his underwear and climbed back onto the bed. Tom always liked to settle himself before sleep by reading a little, but the light was too dim. He squinted at his watch and wondered what time it was back in Melbourne, then gave up. Amanda would be upset he hadn't rung.

* * *

The heat broke a little when rain began to thud onto the metal roof, but it was still very hot and sticky. Tom's skin began to itch, a rash forming first in the palms of his hands, then on his legs and, finally, on the back of his neck.

For weeks now, aspects of his life had been strained. His biggest worry now was Amanda. He sensed his relationship slipping away but, like in a dream, he felt as if he wasn't able to move his arms and legs fast enough to prevent what he saw as inevitable. Amanda hadn't wanted him to come to the Philippines.

'Tom, you're letting your activism get in the way of your academic career,' she'd said as he was leaving. 'And the family,' she'd added, almost as an afterthought.

Amanda was what Tom called a 'university blue-blood'. She'd come from a long line of academics, and The University always came first. Tom felt sure that she had chosen him as her partner principally for love, but realised early in their relationship that his burgeoning academic career would also help continue Amanda's familial institutional line. 'Perhaps it was a mistake to marry a political scientist,' she had once said. 'Far too close to the world of current events.'

He rolled away to the edge of the bed and said his prayers, deliberately but awkwardly *not* using the sign of the cross, which had marked the beginning and the end of so many of his childhood conversations with his God. As Tom got older he had shunned his Catholic upbringing to embrace a 'good atheist' line of belief: There's enough to do in this life, on this Earth, enough wrongs to right, without worrying about sky gods and the life hereafter. But the middle of the night was another thing, a time when the soul exposed its vulnerable underbelly. It was during these times that he prayed for his family, for the dead and those yet to come. He thanked his 'friend' for the gifts of nature, his fortunate life, and he finished his silent soliloquy with the words, 'and please be with the suffering, wherever it is, whatever its form ... be *with* the suffering.'

Tom McMahon was an environmentalist. The suffering was not just that of the human condition, but the very condition of nature itself. It was everywhere, shuddering in every heart, quivering behind every frond in the forest, cracking under every rock. Concerned that his focus on suffering was reaching unhealthy proportions, Amanda had argued with him that there was as much joy in life as there was suffering and that his focus needed to be re-oriented.

'Yes, but the joyous don't need any friends,' had been his curt reply.

Loud snores resonating from beyond the thin walls interrupted his reverie. He tried to think of other things, to imagine that he was not here in this stifling room in a foreign country. He thought of Emily, his four-year-old daughter, blue eyes dancing, running up to him and hugging him when he arrived home. His thoughts drifted to his son Jem, to the football game that he'd managed to find time for the previous weekend.

His children were a source of wonder to him. They were so precious that, strangely, he kept a certain distance from them. Sometimes he felt that if he got too close, something bad would happen and they would break. He did not know the source or cause of this belief. But he feared for them. He feared for them, simply because they were alive. Minor setbacks that they bore — the everyday barbs inflicted upon everyone — took on for him an inflated importance. He wanted to cocoon them, to provide them with a world full of beauty and trust.

He was conscious not to project his anxieties upon them, but these trepidations prevented him from becoming intimately involved in their lives. Amanda was their confidante, their collaborator in daily life. From the children's perspective, their father was someone to admire, but a figure beyond their reach who dealt almost exclusively in a serious world inhabited by grown-ups. On the occasions he did get close they were asleep, tucked up for the night in their beds. He cast himself in the role of invisible protector, a guide watching over them from the threshold of their rooms. At least he could provide the physical and material safety, that steadfastness that he never had as a child.

Amanda was right, he decided. He was tilting at windmills. He wanted to be back in their bedroom, a street lamp throwing light over the high ivy hedge guarding the perimeter of their home, beaming through the stained glass window. He'd always loved the way its distorted mauves and greens mottled his pillow. He wished he was there now, undressing in silence, quietly shuffling into bed with Amanda, staring at the ceiling rosettes. He would love to be with his wife right now, to move into that aromatic place along her neck, to receive her safe embrace.

Instead, he took off his singlet and boxer shorts and lay on his back naked. His throat tightened. He imagined that each waft of air from the communal fan was a zephyr rising from his favourite place: the sea. He thought of the rapid succession of events over the past weeks that had brought him here, when the intermittent rivulets of his life had strengthened and merged into only one ephemeral waterway, floating him towards some single, unavoidable — but, as yet, unknown — landing point.

Gradually, the persistent snores from other cells became unimportant. The steamy Manila night swallowed him, and he dreamed the dream he dreaded most. It was the dream that seemed to visit him when he felt most vulnerable. A dream of a house, not his house with Amanda and the kids. An older house by the sea. In a storm. Fierce, wet winds battered its peeling façade. It was a place of dread. A place he knew he should not enter.

But a voice within told him that he must push on. In the dream he moved through the derelict gate, its rusty hinges seized up long ago through disuse and by the salt air of the sea thumping the cliffs below. A bough from a huge gum tree snapped like the crack of a gun, crashing to the ground directly in front of him. Everything screamed at him that he was not welcome here. In terror, he turned and ran. Back through the gate. Into the night.

2

General Santos City

The steward saw Tom craning his neck over Paul to get a glimpse of the map-like landscape unfolding beneath them, and then explained to him how to use the armrest controls to get a view of the Philippines on the screen in front of him. He'd used this high-tech entertainment gear on some other airlines, but Philippines Air was the first he'd come across with 'landing-gear cam'. No doubt it had been especially designed to capture this wondrous congress of lush green islands, set within a backdrop of the shifting blues of the Indo-Pacific.

Each island appeared miraculously green. Soaring volcanic mountains emerged from the fast low-lying clouds, their bases hidden in a canopy of rainforest. This was a land obviously blessed with water. Even from the air, Tom could see waterfalls hurling themselves outwards, away from the stony precipice of the skyline.

Tom touched Paul on the arm. 'Isn't this incredible?' he asked, over the roar of the engines, which had just begun the aircraft's descent. Paul grinned and nodded.

Tom had warmed to Paul considerably. He wore his legal learning lightly and, despite dwelling in the hothouse of human rights, he seemed calm and considerate. He was a widely travelled man, and it seemed to Tom that Paul had a bigger, more global picture of life than some of his compatriots who had never left the Philippines.

He leaned into Paul, raising his voice to compete with the noise of the propellers whirring on the wing just outside their cabin window.

'You know, a lot of those small islands down there ... might go under if the icecaps continue to melt.'

Paul smiled, scratched his little goatee, and continued to look down at the archipelago, each island encircled by a purple areola of coral. Paul hadn't heard him, Tom thought, so he tried again, this time even louder. 'Some of those low-lying islands. They might disappear soon. You know — climate change?'

'Yes, I hear you, Tom.' But instead of saying anything further on the subject, Paul reached for his earphones, positioning them over his mop of hair. He smiled at Tom one more time, fiddled with the dials in his armrest, found some music, turned it up and thrummed his fingers on his thighs, mouthing the words, 'No woman no cry.' Tom could hear the reggae beat coming through Paul's headset. He then turned towards Maria, sitting across the aisle, to continue his discussion of climate change. But Maria, head down and engrossed in paperwork, made it clear she didn't want to be disturbed by anyone.

Mindanao, the southernmost island in the archipelago, came into view just as night began to fall. The majesty of the place from the air had relieved Tom of some of his tension — particularly since their adventures at Manila's domestic airport terminal earlier that afternoon. The airport police had insisted Mindanao was unfit for Western tourists, and when Tom impulsively blurted out that they were not tourists the police had demanded to know the nature of their business. But Maria came to their rescue, not bothering with explanations relating to the NPO and International Fact-Finding Missions. She'd flashed her Philippines National Radio press pass, which seemed to work wonders. When the police had gone she'd turned to Tom in front of the others and unleashed a withering tirade, mostly in Filipino, but finishing with the words, 'Just keep your mouth shut and let me do the talking.' Paul had politely pretended not to hear.

The Mindanao airport reminded Tom of a crumbling bus station but for one thing: the interior of the entire terminal was encased in another structure of ten-gauge wire. A cage had been welded inside the decrepit concrete building, giving it an air of a prison. The smell of damp and urine overwhelmed him.

They moved to the poorly lit unloading area. No carousels here, just bags dumped onto a concrete floor. 'We'll wait here until Father Ricardo arrives,' Maria said.

While they waited for the priest, Tom gave an Australian dollar coin to a woman carrying a child with no eyes. As this news travelled through the airport, men and women of all ages quickly surrounded Tom. People pulled at his shirt, tugged at his trousers.

'Sir, sir, sir. Please sir, just one dollar.'

'You want girl? Very young. Very clean.'

One powerfully built man shoved him with two fists, making it hard for Tom to stand his ground. He was being pushed back into the wire, with nowhere to go. Others gestured agitatedly, their hands moving to their mouths in mime, begging, he imagined, for pesos or a mouthful of plantain or rice. One woman was so close to him — screaming right in his face — that he felt the heat of her breath and the flecks of spit landing in his eyes. Behind the front row of assault still more bodies pressed, their demands less raw and angry, but mounting a chorus promising anything from tailors, taxis, more sex and even exotic animals.

'Put your filthy money away,' Maria said. 'Handouts will make things worse for them, and for you. They'll get you stabbed. You should know better!' Hissing and growling, she started shooing people away.

After what felt like hours, Father Ricardo appeared. He seemed to manifest miraculously, like a dark-skinned and gritty Moses dressed in a white v-neck shirt, blue shorts and sandals, with an open grin plastered across his broad-boned face. The sea of people bowed, parted and then retreated. Peace and order reigned as Father Ricardo's own entourage encircled him. One was a nun, two wore camouflage-style military fatigues, but the majority wore plain clothes like Ricardo.

'Greetings and blessings, my friends. Welcome to General Santos City!' The priest embraced Maria with surprising affection, planting a huge kiss on her lips. She looked a little awkward — but pleased. He was less demonstrative with Paul but also greeted him as a long-lost friend, slapping him hard on the back, grabbing his shoulders.

'And you must be Dr McMahon,' he said, turning to Tom and shaking his hands warmly. His eyes spoke of a genuine welcome. 'We have been looking forward to your arrival.'

With Father Ricardo by their side they moved freely, leaving the comparative safety of the airport and entering two battered, open-tray trucks that formed part of a convoy. Two military-looking types led the motorcade on motor scooters. There were fewer vehicles on the road than in Manila, but roads were poor and it took them nearly an hour to travel the ten kilometres or so to their destination. Water seeped out from the lush vegetation perched on the verges of the road, lying in pools, puncturing the unmade surface with deep ruts and holes.

The sign above the gate read 'Mindanao Association for Authentic Progress (MAAP)' and under it, in smaller letters, 'People's Environmental Alliance'. The voices of school children rang out from one corner of the compound as they chanted what Tom thought sounded like The Lord's Prayer.

Ricardo explained to his visitors that the compound included a Catholic school for displaced children, as well as the living quarters where the delegates would stay that night. On the northern side was an amenities block, alongside what Ricardo described as a cookhouse. The MAAP offices stood on the eastern side.

The main office reminded Tom of his childhood — it looked just like a six-foot high cubby house. The walls and ceilings were made from masonite, the desks scattered with papers. Tom noticed that a computer, a fax machine and a photocopier took pride of place in one corner, with electric leads running like rivulets across a damp concrete floor. He looked for a place to sit but workers occupied the only chairs in the room, so he had to remain in an upright position with his neck bent uncomfortably at his shoulders, his knees slightly buckled. Several of the workers were similarly stooped, and went about their business without any perceivable inconvenience.

Tom's posture must have looked more ridiculous than Paul and Maria's, however, because when Father Ricardo saw him, he belly-laughed.

'Get the doctor a chair!'

With Tom seated, Ricardo moved into a more serious mode, but continued to smile. 'We are printing up your agenda for the next few days. We will distribute this later. Suffice to say that over the next week you will visit the communities most under threat from the current practices of HMC.'

Ricardo's formal language reminded Tom of the way Enrico had addressed him back in Manila. *Perhaps it has nothing to do with university education*, he thought. *Perhaps they all trained together, honing their language skills to connect with foreign visitors.*

The priest paused and directed that some brochures be passed to Tom. 'Here is a little reading on MAAP and the People's Environmental Alliance. They're people's organisations with close ties to the NPO and other grassroots freedom, human rights and environmental organisations. MAAP also has a close working relationship with some religious institutions operating in Mindanao. It is called the Association for Authentic *Progress* because we are not against progress or development, as long as it is controlled by the people … and it takes place when the people are ready. We call it *authentic* progress because the result of this process enriches the lives of the people, not the pockets of the wealthy. With HMC's Bampakan mine, the people of Mindanao are not yet ready.'

For Tom, again this sounded like the classical Marxist position he'd been belted around the head with at university: once the working class seized the wheels of industry for themselves, everything would be alright. It was markedly different from Tom's Western green position that had fundamental concerns about the nature of industrial progress itself, whoever controlled it. There were only so many resources to go around and often development was not the best option, he felt. He felt flustered by this different position.

He tried to bite his tongue but his interest got the better of him. 'Excuse me, Father Ricardo, may I ask questions if they arise?' he said.

Ricardo looked slightly surprised — he had hardly begun his briefing — but then smiled. 'Of course!'

'Thank you. Is your organisation against open-cut mining?'

'This is a very good question. May I call you Thomas?'

'Please do, Father.'

'MAAP is not against it but, of course, it must be owned by the people in the first place. The people may decide to do things differently. Ultimately, it is not for us, or anyone else, to question the will of the people.' Ricardo turned to a nun standing to his right and said, 'Of course, the Church has a different position to MAAP, and as a priest I have to reconcile these positions.'

He continued calmly — changing tack slightly — but with a conviction that hammered home his original point. 'Mohamed,' he said, facing one of the activists sitting by the photocopier, 'please tell Thomas which organisation you represent.'

'The Muslim Farmer's League,' said the man.

'You see,' said Ricardo, 'this is a very broad umbrella. It is Muslims and Christians working together in our struggle against the Company, against transnational capitalism. All you read about in the Manila papers — and in the Australian press, I might add — is about Mindanao in civil war, a fight between Muslims and Christians. This is far from the truth. It is a fight of the people, for the people of all religions, against the military and the elite. This is the truth of the matter.'

Ricardo moved to a table near the centre of the room which held a map of the main islands of the Philippines. Stuck in the map were innumerable plastic-headed pins of many colours, each depicting a mine. In both Luzon, the main island in the north, and in Mindanao, the pins were so thick on the paper that no other feature could be distinguished.

'The different colours indicate the national identity of the Company's head office, as well as what stage the mining operation is at,' Ricardo said. He touched one of the yellow Australian pins, the dominant colour on the board. 'This pin is Bampakan mine, the major HMC mine we are fighting to close down.'

He moved away from the map, back towards Tom's chair. 'So you see, our friends … this is not just a struggle against HMC, but a fight for our island, our country. And this time, it is transnational corporations who are our most virulent oppressor. Not bandits, not Muslims and not, may I add,' he said with a grin, 'terrorists.'

A woman in a blue bandana appeared at the door of the room, gesturing to the priest with a movement of her hand to her mouth, and he nodded. 'But enough of this for now. You must all be very hungry after your journey. The community has prepared a meal of welcome for you. Please, let us eat in celebration of your safe arrival and to the success of our Fact-Finding Mission.'

Again, Tom had the feeling that most of the priest's address had been stage-managed, a formal pre-rehearsed welcome, probably done many times before. *Others are waiting in the wings to perform their parts, but who is writing the script?* he wondered.

People started filing out of the room, heading towards the cookhouse. In front of it, some teenage boys were playing basketball. Tom had noticed on the way out from the airport how every available open space sported a basketball hoop, some hovering over long grass, others over a patch of balding asphalt or dirt, and most were continually in use. Without hesitating, he took off his shoes and socks, and asked if he could join in. The youths were a bit taken aback at first. His arms towered over the shooters, blocking their path towards the basket, but they moved fast and soon found a way to skirt around him, before executing their liquid-smooth jump shots. He had an advantage because without leaving the ground he could almost touch the hoop, which was lower than the 'legitimate' height. Still, they out-scored him. Tom laughed at the way they made him look like a big galoot, and soon the young men were laughing with him.

Some of the workers came out of the cookhouse, eating their food, when they heard the laughter. A couple of them put down their plates, turned their caps around backwards and joined in. And then it must have been lunchtime for the school as well, because a horde of primary school-aged children began charging towards the basketball court, screaming with delight at the awkward, laughing giant dancing around making a fool of himself.

His fair-skinned face turned beetroot, making him even more comical to the locals. Perspiration fell from his tousled mop of black hair, momentarily blinding him. But he felt fantastic. After days of travel and tension he was *in* his body again. He surged with happiness. He loved children and here he was, surrounded by all these beaming faces.

We really are the same, he thought. Visions of joyous moments with Emily and Jem flooded through him. Grabbing the ball with renewed vigour and purpose, he hurtled towards the ring and leapt with all his might skywards, slamming the ball down through the hoop before losing his balance. He came down on his backside in the dust.

A long silence from the players and the spectators gave way to a roar of laughter, followed by a round of sustained clapping and then more laughter. When he finally arose and began patting off the dust from his pants, he looked up to see both Father Ricardo and Paul bent over from mirth, barely able to gasp for air. Tears poured from their eyes. Through the cloud of dust, Tom noticed that even Maria Cortes had managed a smile.

Paul threw him a towel from his kit bag and Tom sat down on the court, swabbing the sweat from his body. His feet were filthy and he used the towel on them, too.

Jokingly he said, 'I *might* wash it before I give it back to you ... if you're very good.'

Paul punched him gently on the arm in mock anger. One of the men dressed in jungle camouflage offered him a pair of worn down flip-flops. Tom thanked him and went to stand up. But when he did, the children who had moved close to him screamed and retreated in mock fear from the sweaty monster. He warmed to the task, pretending to ignore them and walked towards the cookhouse, noticing out of the corner of his eye that the children were advancing cautiously behind him. He continued to walk, stopped suddenly, turned and yelled like a madman, chasing them, sending them into an absolute frenzy of delight.

After the children withdrew to a safe distance, the most adventurous gingerly began to move closer. Once more he pretended not to notice them, before charging at them, repeating the sequence over and over again.

When finally he moved to the cookhouse, Father Ricardo was waiting for him. Ricardo's smile for him had changed to one of recognition of a fellow traveller. He grabbed him around the shoulders like he had done to Paul at the airport, like an old companion. He shoved a cup of water and a plate of food in front of him and told him to sit down.

'Children, heh? They are our future,' the priest said. His hand became a spoon as he scooped rice into his mouth. 'You know, Thomas, the Filipinos like to touch their food. We like to get *into* it, to feel it before we eat it. No knives and forks here. Look, try moving it to your mouth like this.' It seemed to Tom that the priest had left behind his script — that he was now speaking from the heart.

Tom plunged his hand into the rice. It oozed between his fingers, soft and sticky. Most of it fell from his grasp before it reached his mouth.

'Good, yes? When I watch the American television I think the people must be scared of their food, the way they don't ever lay a hand on it.'

Tom grunted in agreement. Hunger had overtaken him.

'But the rice we eat ... it's inferior. Mindanao is the rice bowl of the Philippines, but all our good rice is exported. But this will do... for now.' He paused, then thought of something else. 'Thomas, do you mind if I ask you some personal questions?'

'Of course not, Father ... shoot.'

'You sometimes work for Horizon Mining Corporation?'

'No, not at all. What gave you that idea?'

'Your Executive Officer has sent me some background materials.'

Bloody Louise, he thought, *what else had she sent him?* From the beginning, she had been set against him coming to the Philippines, and Tom suspected that she would do anything to scuttle this trip. Power-suited and high-heeled, she wore a particularly intense perfume that Tom sometimes imagined was the type they tortured animals to produce.

Although an elected board of volunteers had employed her, Louise Roberts thought she was the most important person in the organisation. She was a career lobbyist who had worked previously for the Liberal Democrats. She cared about the environment in a 'cuddly animal' sort of way, but didn't much care for most environmentalists; she described them as 'fruitloops'.

He realised now that Father Ricardo was staring at him. 'Dr McMahon? It says that you serve on some type of advice-giving committee overseeing the expansion of ... of Moomba Mines. Is that right?'

'Oh, that. Nothing to worry about, really. It's something that my organisation — the Environment Centre — is considering sitting on, along with other stakeholders in the mine's expansion.'

'Stakeholders?'

'Just a fashionable word we use a lot for those with different interests.'

'But you were dealing directly with the Company?'

'Yes, but only as a means to get information. Also, I had to do it as a trade-off to get to the Philippines. You know, there are many ways to skin a cat!'

Ricardo looked puzzled, but continued. 'I am not sure I understand the cat. But I think I understand your position. It is very Western ... I apologise. That was rude of me.'

Despite their camaraderie, their exchanges about mining remained quite formal. He knew some language issues muddied the waters a little, but it was more than this. He felt that the priest was now testing him, with particular responses required.

'Not at all, Father. I am a Westerner, and I'm sure there are many cultural differences in our positions. I'm here to learn. Please always feel free to talk to me openly. Otherwise, my time here will not be spent well.'

'Thank you for saying that, Thomas. I suppose that you are jumping around on shifting sands. Or something to that effect. You Westerners pursue every pathway at once. We prefer to learn the lessons each pathway provides before moving on to the next one. How is wisdom attained if there is no progression?'

'It's a good question, Father. I think I'm gradually learning that our approach doesn't always work in the long run. Not everyone is everyone else's friend. There may be a need to identify an enemy, on occasions.'

Tom felt that in his own culture, every pathway, every opinion received equal weight. In some ways, his own Environment Centre's dealing with the Company was based on this position, or non-position. Sometimes he had referred to it as the 'universal embrace': every which way must be pursued simultaneously, without judgement.

'Well said. But are you still on this company's committee?' Ricardo persisted.

'Haven't decided yet. I know the Company wants to use the process to legitimate its own status. But it's been very useful in terms of me understanding the Company's position — its mindset. I'd justify involvement on that basis alone.'

Father Ricardo stared into his bowl, seeming to temporarily lose his appetite, swirling and flicking the rice absent-mindedly between his index finger and thumb. There was a small silence between them and Tom dispelled it quickly. 'Please Father, as I've already said … please feel free to speak your mind in front of me.'

'Of course. But I am reticent to say this … because this is not a trifling issue. I already believe you to be a good man. Your people and God have set you on this path for a purpose. But you must understand that I disagree with you at the most fundamental level. We can never deal with the Company, here in the Philippines or anywhere else. The people only have one real source of power, and that is their community, their solidarity. Without this, we are dead. Instead, we must resist as a combined force. I say "resist" — not negotiate or reform. For this reason, we do not deal with or even recognise the Company — it has no face for us.' The priest began eating again, but this did not slow his speech in any way. 'You may know that we are a peasant nation?'

'Yes, Enrico from the NPO gave me a basic demography lesson yesterday. He seemed very proud of the fact.'

'Ah, Enrico. A passionate man. And he is right some of the time. There are many good things to cherish in the peasant's life, particularly if he is attached to some land. But of course, more and more Filipinos are losing their land, however small, and are plunged into a horrible existence, the life of the shadow, the life of the living dead.

'We spend most of our time mobilising … educating the people about mining. Just last month we drove a group of chieftains up to the Singuet Mines in the north of the island and showed them what 'open-cut' actually means. They stared into the gaping hole in the earth for the first time. You must realise, Thomas, that they have never witnessed anything like this — on such a massive scale — even in their wildest dreams. The chieftains consulted with each other for a long time. Finally, Chief Abulu, one of the oldest and most respected, asked me some questions on their behalf. He spoke in a local indigenous dialect so it's hard to convey the exact meaning, but he said something like this: "Have the Holy Mountains been taken by the clouds or have they fallen into the abyss?" I told him that the Company had taken the mountain for its own purpose, to make things of metal. He then asked, "But how much metal do they want?" I told him and the other chieftains that the Company's yearning for metal knew no bounds. The chieftains could not understand the concept of desire without limits.'

The priest pushed his plate aside and took a ladle to fill Tom's cup with water. Tom didn't dare ask if it was safe to drink. This was the universe beyond bottled water. Then suddenly, someone yelled out to the priest from inside the office and he made movements to suggest the conversation was over.

'I will not say any more on this issue now. No doubt you and I have much to talk about in relation to the world, its people and all creation. But Thomas, you will not be dealing with the Company here. The powerless cannot *deal* with the powerful. You will confuse people and they will not trust you. Please don't mention your involvement in your *committee* or your dealings with HMC to anyone else. They will not understand.' He took both Tom's hands again and shook them warmly. 'I'm glad we've had this conversation.'

And with that, he disappeared into the office.

* * *

The priest's enquiries had touched a nerve. After Ricardo departed, Tom was left to eat the remainder of his meal alone. He realised he'd had too little time to reflect upon these important strategic issues, to digest events that had occurred in a kind of whirlwind over the past month.

Dealing with the Company, even at the level of information gathering, had also caused some rifts back in Australia.

Although no-one's position, even the eco-warriors', had been as hard-and-fast as Ricardo's, Tom thought. He remembered a meeting at the Environment Centre in the week leading up to his departure for the Philippines. Louise had ambushed him by inviting a delegation from HMC — including the CEO, Roger Rumley — who were interested in funding a special edition of the Centre's magazine on sustainability and mining.

'Oh, Tom. You're here already,' she'd greeted him when he'd arrived at the Centre on one of his regular Tuesday mornings. Dressed in a cream suit, her highly manicured appearance was incongruous in the shabby surroundings. The Centre was stuck together with lick and spittle, furniture gracing the place after it had long ceased being useful in others, pieces of ill-matching carpet and tape reaching up to grip and catch unaware feet. Turning back to her mobile phone, she had mumbled something and hung up. Moving towards his office, she had greeted him with a firm handshake. She had been slightly more distant with him of late.

Suddenly, the front doorbell had rung and in walked Patrick Walters. *This should be interesting,* Tom thought. *It looks like some of the climate change and anti-uranium activists have got wind of the meeting with Rumley.*

'Shit,' said Louise, her calm cracking suddenly. 'Bloody Walters is here!'

One of the activists she despised most was Patrick Walters. With short-cropped white hair and thick bottle-top glasses, Walters always dressed casually in jeans and an open-necked cheese-cloth shirt. He was a movement superstar. Tom couldn't count the number of times Patrick had been arrested, but several instances came readily to his mind: he'd been thrown in gaol for blockading bulldozers naked in the rainforest at Errinundera Plateau; for throwing frozen cage chickens at the leader of the state opposition as he walked up the steps at Parliament House; and, most memorably, for surfing the bow-wave of a US nuclear destroyer as it cruised through the Heads into Port Philip Bay. He had worn a placard over his green wet-suit saying, 'Break the Carbon and Nuclear Fuel Cycles!'

He didn't even brush his teeth due to what he understood as 'the military-industrial complex fluoride conspiracy'. Both his breath and his take-no-prisoners attitude offended many.

Louise continued, 'I knew he'd ruin the deal!'

'What deal?'

In her sudden anger, Louise had uncharacteristically blurted out more information than necessary. 'Oh, you know, the meeting with Rumley.'

'Two things, Louise,' Tom responded coolly. 'First, I didn't mention my meeting with Rumley to anyone except you. And, secondly, a meeting is a long way off from a deal.'

'Listen, it's vital that you cut Walters off at the pass. We should at least give them the courtesy of hearing them out without white noise blasting across the table from bloody radicals. I'll go out the front and show Rumley's entourage into the boardroom. Give me two minutes … and then you go and re-arrange a time with Walters.'

'Send them into the boardroom, Louise,' retorted Tom wearily.

'Sorry? Which ones exactly?'

'All of them.'

Almost immediately the visitors made their way to the boardroom — Walters in tow, eyes flashing, his mouth set in a sneer. Tom gestured to the boardroom table that had once belonged in his kitchen. 'Sit down, everyone,' he muttered.

Rumley was no fool, but Tom imagined he was also fairly unfamiliar with situations like this. He would be used to tightly controlled agendas, working best in the glitzy backrooms of large transnational hotels. Tom had only seen him briefly in the past, surrounded by a coterie of pallid-faced, middle-aged men who looked, thought, dressed and lived just like Rumley himself. Face-to-face contact with some of the very antagonists who had given his company so much grief over the past several years was something he wouldn't expect.

After Tom's introductions, Rumley's Public Relations Manager, Jenny Thompson, kicked the conversation off, cracking her fingers briefly as if preparing for battle. She was as polished to look at as Louise, although Tom sensed a real hardness about her, impenetrable under her silky-smooth exterior.

'We've decided that the environment is no longer a constraint to our business, our profitability. Rather, good environmental practices make good business sense in the medium to long term. We, at HMC, like to think of ourselves as sustainable developers. We'd like to bury the hatchet, to recognise that in the past we may have been a little defensive towards environmental concerns. We believe that there is a lot of scope for working together in the future ... that by working together, benefits may accrue to both our brands.'

'Now wait a minute ...' Walters spluttered, as if chewing on a nasty piece of gristle. 'We're not a brand. We're a movement. A movement of people dedicated to stopping corporations like yours from desecrating the planet, from destroying our Earth. We're not into profits. We do what we do because we believe we *must* ... for all of the Earth and for future generations.'

Tom and Louise exchanged uneasy glances.

'Mr Walters, don't get us wrong,' she continued curtly. 'We know you are very committed people. But we believe that there may be opportunities on both sides, if both organisations recognise what is common to their positions rather than what is different.'

'Give us an example,' said Louise, her request suspiciously on cue. Tom wondered if anyone else in the room had picked up on this 'effortless' flow of question and answer.

Rumley took his cue from his PR director. 'We believe, at HMC, that in order to make our mining facilities *best practice*, in terms of climate change and sustainable development, then we have to involve environmentalists. In this vein, we'd like to contribute $40,000 for a special edition on mining in your excellent journal, *Environmental*

Options.' He looked directly at Louise.

'Wonderful,' cried Louise, feigning surprise and delight.

'We think that this is a good example of twenty-first century environmentalism,' Rumley continued. 'Not done by sitting in front of bulldozers, or swinging from trees, but working together — a partnership between government, business and the third sector. This will result in a win-win-win situation.' He paused, and then added, 'Of course, we'd also like to be involved in the production of the special mining edition.'

Tom knew that although such sums of money were small fry in large corporate and government circles, they were huge within the context of the Environment Centre's budget. He decided to pull in the conversation a bit.

Looking Rumley in the eye, he said, 'Mr Rumley, this is a very generous package. Obviously something of such magnitude can't be decided upon in a small meeting such as this. This is definitely something for the full Board of Management to discuss. And the next meeting of the voluntary Board ... I think, is—'

'Really, Dr McMahon. Perhaps it's not necessary to worry the Board,' Louise cut in. 'It's not really a policy decision, simply an auxiliary financial matter which can be dealt with executively.'

Before Tom could rally, put his Executive Officer in place and exert his presidential authority over proceedings, Louise chimed in again. 'This is a wonderful opportunity for *Environmental Options*. We've been looking to do an edition on green mining for some time.'

'Oh, *green mining* — I like that!' the Jenny Thompson sang out. 'That could be the marketing banner for the edition. In many ways that makes sense. In the last few years we see ourselves more as farmers rather than what has traditionally been understood as "mining". Creating microclimates in all types of habitats, ultimately leading to a carbon-friendly and sustainable environmental future. We want to focus on the positive environmental stories, like our program to look after the stick-nest rat habitats near the mines sites.'

Tom then noticed that Walters had steadily worked himself up into a sweat. He noticed white spittle forming at the corners of Walter's mouth, framing two bloodless, cracked lips.

'*Green mining*, hey?!' Walters spat, causing Tom to shoot him a warning look. 'No, hear me out. It's my turn. No mention of uranium, then? Not a word about your role in the nuclear fuel cycle? And what about your plutonium and other high-level processed wastes? Toxic materials with a longer shelf life than Walt Disney's cryogenically suspended head! I suppose you'll be wanting no mention of the mines next? Or the indigenous peoples they displace? That you dig bloody great holes in the earth — our home — and dump your poisonous slurry into bloody great tailings dams built with about as much engineering longevity as an aboveground pool! No mention, I suppose, that you draw down millions of litres of water every bloody day from the Artesian Basin, destroying the mound springs in the desert, without paying so much as a red cent to the bloody government or the communities that live there!' With this last comment, he swivelled in his chair to direct his blast at Louise. 'And as for you—'

'Now Patrick, let's keep this civil,' ordered Tom sharply.

Patrick took no notice. 'As far as I'm concerned — and I speak for all the members of Critical Mass — you can shove their stick-nest rat right up your arse!'

With that, he had pushed over one of the grey partitions that separated the boardroom from the rest of the open-plan meeting area, and stormed out of the building.

* * *

Now, basking in the sunshine of Mindanao, Tom stared down at a small ball of rice he'd moulded unconsciously in his right hand. The fragrance of moist frangipanis sluiced through him. He laughed out loud about the environmental award which his own organisation — driven largely by Louise — had since granted HMC for their protection of the stick-nest rat, probably just to spite Patrick Walters.

What a narrow notion of the environment HMC were selling, he thought. It was the same one that many of the more moderate and powerful greenies in his own group were now swallowing, without question. What had happened to the idealistic movement for change that he had so enthusiastically joined twenty years ago? *Perhaps Walters was right*, Tom thought. *Maybe we've become just a brand after all.*

3

Bampakan

The rear of the bus had no suspension at all. Since leaving MAAP's compound in General Santos City at dawn the previous morning, Tom had bounced and shuddered over every pothole in the road that stretched out towards the westernmost parts of the island. It was still early in the season for monsoonal rains, but already the roads were in disarray. In his own country, he would not have attempted to traverse this terrain without a four-wheel drive. But here they were in an old school bus, often in mud up to its gunnels, labouring towards the foothills of the remote western mountain range. Maria had just informed them they were still another hour away from the place where they planned to spend the night.

Very early the previous morning in General Santos City, an agenda for the members of the International Fact-Finding Mission had been posted on a pinboard, just outside MAAP's main office. It had taken Tom some time to register that he was the sole reason why the Mission was referred to as 'international'. The rest of the troupe comprised Father Ricardo, Maria, Paul and a changing number of drivers and soldier-types he was rarely introduced to. For the next five days the schedule would be relentless. They would be travelling to both the mines and the communities affected by them. Bampakan was first: the town closest to HMC's major copper and gold mine on the island. Eventually, they would journey further up into the highlands, to meet with a B'laan tribe, who just had their mountain earmarked for HMC's next exploratory mine.

Not long after sundown, the bus lurched to a stop in a clearing by the side of the road. The driver attached heavy tarpaulins to the side and then tied these off to a dense copse of trees that marked the beginnings of the tropical forest. The priest lit a fire and prepared a basic dinner of boiled rice and fish. They ate in relative silence as rainbow-coloured birds and colossal insects thickened the dusk. The smoke kept some of the mosquitoes away from under the tarpaulin, but the hardy ones weren't deterred.

Throughout the night, Tom woke with the buzzing. He slapped pointlessly at the air and his body and heard the others doing the same. Sleep was proving impossible. In frustration, he lay his tweed jacket on the ground, providing some relief for hips and shoulders.

His sleeping bag was too hot to lie in even though they slept in the open, but if he slept on top of it the mosquitoes ravaged him. *Thank Christ for the jacket*, he thought. It was funny how new circumstances changed the order and purpose of things.

He'd been erratic in taking his anti-malarial medication and this worried him. But worse than the bugs and the discomfort of sleeping rough was the traffic noise. During the day they had been the only ones on the road, but at night the roads were dominated by freight vehicles. Large trucks thundered past their makeshift camp hour after hour, spewing diesel and lead-enriched exhaust into the verges of the forest.

He noticed Paul trying to light a mosquito coil with a match, but the humidity wouldn't allow it to ignite. Tom remembered he had a disposable lighter in his backpack and soon they managed to light the coil, hovering over its smoke side by side. Spending so much time together over the past few days — first in Manila, and then in General Santos — had made them closer. To be in each other's company in the middle of a strange, sleepless night offered some solace to both of them. And the night was no place for small talk, its darkness providing the opportunity for more intimate conversation to emerge from daytime hiding.

Paul went straight to the heart of the matter. 'So you haven't told me why you're here yet. I mean, I know it makes strategic sense and all that political stuff you go on about ... taking on the corporations in a transnational fashion. Most of it I agree with by the way, but what really brings, you know ... what brings *Tom McMahon* here?'

Tom usually felt very uncomfortable participating in such introspection, particularly when the spotlight shone on him. 'Navel gazing' he called it. Psychological bullshit. People disappearing up their own sphincters, fascinated only by their own motivations and little else. Tom knew his inability to trust, to truly share his life, was based on his inability to expose his fears, his weaknesses. He was in a permanent state of battle-readiness. He knew life was complex, that actions were informed by a myriad of reasons and non-reasons, that his childhood may have hardened him, distanced him from intimacy. And no sooner had he invoked this troubled past, as so often happened, an image of his father flashed before him, all red face and veiny forearms. But he shook it away, cast it out before it could take root. His childhood *could* be construed positively, he'd often thought. It had given him a tough edge around a soft heart, and had cast his outlook beyond the world which floated directly in front of him.

But on this remote night, in these extreme circumstances, he felt the beginnings of wanting to open up a little bit. 'I suppose normally I don't like to explain away political involvement on the basis of personal experience. Too often we're told that political engagement is not *normal* ... that we must be sick bastards, or emotionally and psychologically scarred before we will engage. I tell my students that being political should be the norm. Not some kind of pathological response.'

'Yes ... could be. I already told you, Tom. I did my law degree in Australia. That's where I first heard the terms 'shit-stirrers' and 'muckrakers' ... you know, to describe activists. So I see where you're coming from. But can't it be more complex than just one or the other? I mean, can't there be shit that happens in your own life that makes you passionate about things? You know ... about specific political issues.'

Tom saw an opportunity to shift the focus. 'So, is that why you became a lawyer?'

'Oh, you know. There's always more than one reason why we do anything. Sure, growing up in one of the poorer parts of Manila was a pretty good intro to powerlessness. Something I promised myself I'd get stuck into when I grew up. Some of it was probably just pride or ego. Westerners aren't the only ones with an ego, you know! I chased success like anyone else. I got the marks, so I did law. And it was a chance to get out of the Philippines for a while. See how others lived. But yeah, I rationalised that if I could get legal training then I'd be able to contribute ... to help, where it was needed.'

The coil burnt out and mosquitoes, midges and other insects immediately recommenced their attacks. The two men wrestled with the lighting of another coil. Now even the lighter would not spark properly in the saturated atmosphere. It took a full five minutes to light.

Paul took out a pack of chewing gum and offered a stick to his new ally. Tom found the peppermint taste oddly comforting, a scent and flavour from his own world.

'Anyway, enough about me. I was asking the questions. Remember?' Paul said.

'My apologies, Counsel,' grinned Tom.

'C'mon Tom. Give me something to pin you on. Are you a Catholic?'

Looking around the camp, Tom checked to see that the others were asleep. It seemed they were, though some bodies were rotating on a rotisserie of sweat and discomfort.

'I was when I was a little kid,' Tom said. 'Used to go to church until

I was about ten.'

'There you are,' said Paul. 'We know all about Catholicism in the Philippines! Once a Catholic always a Catholic. All that guilt. They got you early then!'

'I don't know about that guilt stuff. If it's true, then it's probably not a bad thing to have. I mean, you know, all that about mercy. I think I did get influenced by that a fair bit. Compassion for the weak and the suffering. Perhaps that's part of why I'm here.'

Paul wasn't satisfied with his answer. 'But you seem to turn everything into an intellectual argument.' Paul lay down, turned on his side facing Tom and rested his head back on a makeshift pillow. Tom lit a third coil. For no perceptible reason it was easier this time.

'Why did you stop going to church?' Paul asked.

'Oh, I don't know. My churchgoing probably just coincided with my time at the orphanage. I was nearly five when I went there, and left when I was ten to go and live with my grandparents. And they weren't churchgoing types, so that was the end of it.'

'Orphanage?'

'Yeah. I don't like to talk about it much. Doesn't achieve anything.' Tom sighed, but continued. 'It all started when my brother Sean and I were farmed out to some distant cousins in the bush. Mum couldn't look after us anymore. She'd ended up in hospital with a breakdown that she never came out of ... until her end. Well, that was what everyone told me at the time. So Aunt Josephine, Mum's sister, sort of hid us for a while. For a few months, I reckon. Anyway, Dad eventually found out where we were and took us home. Sean was small — still a baby really — and I was only a couple of years older. Probably just about to turn four.'

Tom found himself thinking back to those earlier times. He remembered that he'd found a brief happiness at Aunt Josephine's in the form of a hobby-horse on wheels. He'd ridden it all around the rose garden. But one morning, while he was down collecting the eggs, his Dad's blue Holden had come up the driveway. Even the wheels of his car were angry. His father had grabbed Tom roughly, while Sean stood there crying. Tom yelled, 'Aunt Josephine! Help! He's here! He's got me! Please, don't let him take me!' His dad had held Tom high, legs cart-wheeling in the air.

'Oh, Dad. Please let me stay here,' he'd cried, looking directly at his father for the first time that day. 'Take Sean ... you can have Sean.' Tom remembered the smell of his father's breath, the strong fumes of stale beer mixed with Craven A cigarettes. Tom loved his brother but he would have fed Sean to the wolves one hundred times over if that meant he could escape his father's grasp.

* * *

Paul sat stroking his wispy goatee, preening individual strands of hair between his fingers. Tom noticed a gentleness about him, a willingness to listen. He was surprised how easy it felt to tell him these things.

'So we spent the next year with Dad living in the caravan. He'd lost his job and had to rent the house out. To say he'd stopped coping ... well, he'd always been an alcoholic. But I suppose life with Mum, however rough, had provided a bit of stability for him. In the end he just lost it, I think. Just bolted. One of my uncles, Bert, said he'd seen him up in Brisbane. But that was all we heard of him.'

'Is that when you went to the orphanage?'

'Yeah. Shit of a place. One of those bluestone prisons for children run by the nuns.'

'What was the worst thing about it?'

'Well Paul ... or do you want me to call you Freud? Or are you of a neo-Jungian persuasion?'

Paul laughed a little too loud and a couple of the bodies stirred. 'No, you're the doctor. I was just interested, that's all.'

Tom thought for a good while more, staring at patterns of smoke rising from the coil into the overhanging boughs of the trees, trying to decipher letters and words formed within the rising rings.

'The worst thing was not being able to see Sean.'

He pictured the huge staircase winding into the clouds, the railings high over his head. He remembered creeping up the steps one at a time, quietly. Nearly at the top ... then, bang! Something had hit him in the back of the head.

'What do you think you're doing up here, you naughty boy?' yelled the nun.

'I want to see Sean,' he said defiantly. The woman seemed huge, but he hated her and hate sometimes gave strength, even to little boys.

'I've told you before, Thomas, you're not allowed in the nursery.'

'But I want to see my brother,' he answered. She hit him again, sending him to bed without dinner.

The sickly smell of boiled sausages and vanilla custard came into the dormitory from the dining hall, as he lay quietly on his bed.

Then at night, when the bunkroom lights were turned off, the crying of the other children started. But he refused to give in, to let them win. He never cried.

Every day he sat on the tucker box out the front of the orphanage. *Why are you taking so long, Mummy?*

He hadn't properly thought of these events in years, and was surprised by the lump forming in his throat. 'Enough cross-examination for one night, Paul. We better get some shut-eye.'

Tom plumped up his tweed jacket and tried to settle down again. Trucks continued their deafening arpeggios as they climbed and descended, and in between their noisy approaches and departures, the raucous symphony of the insect world filled the night. Just before nodding off, he noticed a cigarette's bright orange glow lighting up Marias' furrowed face.

* * *

It was just on dusk when they entered the Diocese of Carbel. The bus finally climbed up the last of the foothills at the entrance to Bampakan. The small town cowered in evening shadows cast by two huge mountains, one enclosed by profuse forest, the other logged clean.

Maria had sat next to Tom all day, her officious iciness noticeably softening. She commented on the features, both historical and geological, that had whirred past their window. She wove stories of Mindanao's land and people into her descriptions, her usual frown spontaneously replaced by ripples of childlike wonder. This gentler, less harried version of Maria revealed a woman of uncommon intelligence. Occasionally she spoke into her handheld tape recorder, a rare reminder that she was also a journalist, though her roles, like most other people Tom had met in the Philippines, seemed blurred.

She told Tom the story of the B'laan people of Mindanao. It was a tale of invasion, resettlement, invasion alongside resettlement, more invasion and the final dispossession and devastation.

'First came the Spaniards, then the Americans and then the Australians,' she said. She described the huge transnational forestry and plantation corporations who had hacked vast holes into dense forests, replacing them with endless mono-cultured fields of genetically engineered crops destined for the mouths of non-Filipinos.

'And then came the mining companies like HMC,' she continued, who had burrowed into sacred mountains, digging enormous open-pit mines with toxic wastes housed in primitive tailings dams, leaching into the source waters of rivers, poisoning them as soon as clouds touched the earth.

'The B'laan,' Maria said, 'have now been pushed off the plains and are taking refuge bit by bit, higher and higher in the mountains.'

These people were clutching onto the edge, a sheer drop confronting them. Nowhere else to go — within a whisper of the decimation of their culture, the imminent burning and scattering of the tap-roots of their community.

'When the HMC entered the picture,' said Maria, shaking her head, 'they discovered the second-biggest copper deposit in Asia in the B'laan's mountain.'

It was after midday that Maria honed in on the most pressing issue before the Mission. 'The Company has managed to split the indigenous communities over here.'

'How?' Tom asked.

'Well, a couple of things came out of their Australian bag of tricks. You know, divide-and-conquer tactics: casting doubts over tribal ownership, confusing boundaries. Plus some others. They're using the same crowd of anthropologists and geographers that they used up at Moomba in South Australia — a company called Access International.'

'Nice name.'

Maria looked over the top of her reading glasses. Her seemingly bottomless brown eyes fixed him in a stare. Tom realised then that she might not have a sense of humour around these matters.

'What they've done in the Philippines is a little more sophisticated,' Maria said. 'The way the legislation was drawn up, the Company had to get the signatures of seven chieftains on their Memoranda of Agreement. To get them to sign, the Company promised all sorts of things: education, jobs, health and wealth beyond their imagination. They even had a cartoon drawn up to show the "before" and "after". With cavemen on the left, you know, living in the dark, and then another series of cartoons on the right — after they've signed the agreement — living in computerised luxury. Well, Access had a problem. Only three of the chieftains would sign. So they came up with what they thought was a brilliant idea. They disputed the legitimacy of the chieftains' rule, saying that it was *undemocratic.*'

'You're joking,' Tom said. Then he immediately reminded himself that she didn't kid around.

'It gets better. So the next thing is they hold an election. Of course, the four dissenting chieftains don't turn up. The government says, "Alright. You've had your chance. You didn't vote, so we'll deal with the democratic ones, the ones that have signed the agreement." The tribal communities lose all their decision-making structures, all their power, setting tribe against tribe.'

This rang bells for Tom. He remembered what Patrick Walters had once said back in Australia. HMC had managed to divide and rule the indigenous communities in Australia as well, but this push for absolute ownership of the tribal lands just seemed too brutal to be true.

Now they were entering the outskirts of Bampakan and Maria was telling him that the mountain without trees was the site of the currently operating HMC mine, also named Bampakan, after the township. The other mountain — slightly higher and still wooded — was called Mossy Mountain. It was the proposed site of a newer, larger mine. This was the HMC's digging ground for the largest copper deposits in Asia.

'You can see how the forest clearances have led to more run-off,' she said. 'See how the river has gouged into the flood plain, all the fallen trees choking it up.'

Tom nodded. He felt exhausted now, but her voice soothed him, despite the devastation it described. As the river whirred past them, his thoughts shifted back to another river. With Maria's voice crooning in the background, he recalled his father fishing on the banks of the Murray.

'Tom, don't go too close to the water,' his father had barked.

He remembered his dad reclining in the shade of a large red gum, his eyes closed, his head rested on the old foam Esky that he seemed to take everywhere. His fishing rod dangling in the eddying river. The gnarled limbs of a gum tree cast mesmerising shadows onto the water. Tom thought he could see a cow. Or was it a man? And then he saw a monster in the water, but he knew he would get into trouble if he woke his father.

He decided to climb the tree to get a better look. The rough bark skinned his knees but Tom didn't care. He loved to climb. People had often told him he was a good climber. Higher he went, his bare toes becoming part of each branch. He leaned out over his dad.

From here he could see the causeway they had come across. And somewhere across this land bridge lay his mother. 'Oh Mummy … please come back,' he whispered above the shifting of the leaves and the murmurings of the river.

Holding his breath, he inched along the lightest, the greenest of limbs. *What's that?* he thought, staring into the depths. The monster began to move towards him. Fear forced his hands open and Tom plummeted into the water.

He still remembered the blackness as he sank deeper and deeper towards the muddy bottom, his eyes riveted open, staring up towards the surface of the river, towards the light. Expecting the monster to come, he was sure he was going to die.

A noise from above. Bubbles everywhere. Two big red hands reaching out and then engulfing him.

His dad wrapped him roughly in the car blanket. Even though he spoke crossly, his noxious breath comforted Tom. His dad's money had got all wet, so he hung it out to dry. He gave Tom a big hug, and Tom had momentarily forgotten the terrifying river bottom. And then he lashed Tom hard over the backs of his legs with his belt.

Tom still remembered feeling so much of his father's guilt and failure in that moment. This mixture of emotion was like a bittersweet elixir to the little boy. At four years of age he already knew the meaning of tragic: his dad.

* * *

The Diocese compound was not really a compound at all. *No high-level security here*, Tom thought, staring absently out of the window of the food hall. He noticed how the razor-wired walls of Manila had been replaced with squat mudbrick fences.

Tom glanced over at the parish priest who had hosted their dinner. *He must be no older than mid-thirties*, Tom thought. After everyone had lingered over their food and attempts at light conversation, Tom saw the priest abruptly signal everyone to depart. They shuffled into the meeting hall, attached to the eastward wing of an old church. Here, members of the Fact-Finding Mission met with the President of the Laity — Mr Diego — who chaired the meeting. Silver-haired and with a deeply burnished face, he was much older than the parish priest. He took control of the meeting immediately, calling all to order in a chocolate baritone, a voice of unquestioned authority. Despite not having taken holy orders, it seemed to Tom that he possessed quite a deal of power.

After opening statements from the president, the parish priest, the curate who was in charge of political affairs and Father Ricardo, an array of local people were introduced to the IFFM. Tom originally thought they were just going to sit around for a chat after dinner but this was more like a quasi-judicial hearing, with witnesses apparently to be cross-examined by members of the Mission. He glanced over at Maria who, with her recorder running, was gnawing the inside of her cheek in concentration and vigorously scribbling down all of the testimonies regarding the mine. He almost laughed at Paul's efforts to pay close attention, as Paul struggled to keep his eyes open after a night of zero sleep.

In an attempt to gain some symbolic balance at least, the chair of the meeting introduced alternating witnesses for and against the mine. One of the most interesting testimonies of the evening came from Pedro Manuel, brother of Bampakan's mayor, who was very much on the Company's side. He presented the panel with an array of public relations documents that looked very familiar to Tom, sporting the Company's logo in the red, white and blue. Manuel, a portly man with a handlebar moustache, ran the Community Consultative Committee. He was also the deputy president — his brother Julio, the president — of the grandiosely entitled Independent Scientific Monitoring Committee. Tom read from the brochure:

'The ISMC ensures that the effects of the Bampakan Mine are monitored by local residents, without fear or favour from HMC. In this manner, we can be assured of the highest levels of objective analysis, carried out by the people themselves.'

As he fingered through the colour documents describing the scientific monitoring process, he faced Manuel squarely.

'Mr Pedro Manuel. I'm very interested in the collation of scientific data by your committee. May I ask a few questions? Perhaps I can learn from you? Maybe there are lessons for my own country?'

Manuel beamed with pleasure. 'Of course, Dr McMahon.'

'Who is on this committee?'

Immediate mutterings of discontent broke out around the table, even among members of the panel who Tom knew to be against the continued operation of the mine and its future expansion. After some time, silence fell over the humid, open-windowed room.

Manuel began his response in careful English. 'People from our own Bampakan community … the mayor, myself, two farmers and two mine workers.'

'May I ask if any of you have any scientific training?'

Again, the people at the table rumbled and frowned. This time it was the President of the Laity, Mr Diego, who responded on Pedro Manuel's behalf. 'Dr McMahon, we have not all had the opportunities for education that perhaps you have.'

Many at the table nodded in agreement and, sensing this, Manuel's resolve strengthened visibly, and he resumed his own testimony. 'We are simple, honest and — how do you say — working-hard people, Dr McMahon. Trained with tools at the parish school. We gather this … this information and send it away. We only measure basic things, like water in our streams.'

'Please, Mr Manuel. Don't take offence at my line of questioning. I am only interested in how this process works. I am not querying your committee's integrity or competence.'

Manuel, whether he fully understood the substance of Tom's comments or not, seemed momentarily appeased and nodded.

'Thank you for your generosity and understanding,' Tom continued. 'I only have two more brief questions. In the decade of the mine's operation, has the Scientific Committee produced any basic data which questions facets of the mine's operation?'

But again, Diego interrupted: 'All our tests support the fact that HMC operates at the highest, most technologically advanced and environmentally sustainable levels.' The president of the lay community sounded exactly like one of the brochures Manuel was carrying.

But isn't the Church against the mine? Tom wondered. *Perhaps only part of the Church is opposed to it.*

'Thank you, Chair. And finally, Mr Manuel,' asked Tom, 'which party provides the final scientific analysis of the raw data provided by your independent committee?'

Any attempts by Tom to soften the mood of the meeting evaporated. All participants knew the answer: the Company monitored itself. The Filipinos looked quite shocked by Tom's directness. After an audible, sharp intake of breath, even Father Ricardo looked taken aback. Apparently Tom had crossed some invisible line, broken some basic cultural rule.

Again, it took some time before Manuel gathered his thoughts. He said something in the local dialect and the president nodded in vigorous agreement. The single rattan fan whined unevenly overhead. Huge mosquitoes roamed freely in and out of the room.

'Dr McMahon,' began Diego's sonorous voice. 'The Philippines is a wonderful but very poor nation. The Church and our government are very happy when their burden is shared by others. I'm sure you will understand it does not have the means to provide analysis of every stream, every mine. HMC has been good enough to provide this service.'

With those comments, Diego cut short any further questioning from Tom. For the second time that day, he thought of Patrick Walters and his performance at the Environment Centre. He remembered trying to silence him at the ill-fated meeting back in Australia, but now understood a little more how he must have felt. Tom shocked himself by identifying with him. There was a time when Patrick's actions had seemed so completely off-the-wall.

Many of the people who were called to provide evidence offered very little: a few phrases about why the mine should or shouldn't go ahead; some descriptions of the benefits to, or impacts upon, the community. Nothing new, nothing unheard of before. This struck Tom as some form of theatre, with lines of dialogue agreed upon previously by all parties, and him being the only one without the script.

Knowing that he would not be called on again, Tom's mind wandered back to his home in Melbourne. He hadn't been able to ring Amanda or the kids yet and he knew the chances of getting to a phone were pretty slim. Every day took him further from the possibility. He kicked himself for not ringing while still in mobile phone range. He imagined how their reunion would soon be, stringing together images from a hundred past homecomings until a perfect moving picture played within him. He remembered how, after a long afternoon of classes and appointments, he would set off for home on the 249 bus, which worked its way south-eastwards, through the inner bayside suburbs of Melbourne. In his mind's eye, it was just past dusk, the first fragrances of darkness settling over his street. Musty leaves and the rotting golden berries of white cedars rustled at his feet. In his childhood, they had burned in piles by the side of the road, seasonal incense washing through games of street football and lodging in jumpers and overcoats.

Tom remembered moving silently along the footpath, feeling warmed as he looked through neighbours' windows, sensing the evening regimen unfolding within these solid homes: dinner preparation, bathtime, children doing homework, watching the evening news. He had felt safe in its midst.

Before opening the gate of his own home, he would stand still for a while, motionless in mind and body for the first time that day. He often looked admiringly at his home. Its thick stone veranda posts were slightly narrower at the top. They flared outwards as they reached their tessellated tiled roots, fixed resolutely in the ground. Built in the 1920s, this was a responsible house, a home of substance. It was squat but large, heavy in its stone and brickwork. Around this sturdiness were flashes of colour and quaint Lloyd-Wright designs. Bay windows, framed with stained glass, filtered the internal light. Rose gardens separated the house from the streetscape, punctuated by the ghostliness of three silver birches.

In his mind's eye, his feet crunched along the path to the front door, and he exhaled the stale air that had been sitting at the bottom of his lungs all day. Once inside, he moved up along the passageway, pausing for a moment where the hallway bent into the shape of an 'L'. He loved this spot — the peaceful spine of the house. No sooner had he entered than shrieks of delight moved rapidly down the hallway. He dropped his satchel as Emily hurtled towards him, screaming, 'You're home!'

Home.

He slapped at a mosquito stinging the back of his neck and looked around the meeting hall. It was now ten o'clock, and there were still six more witnesses on the typed agenda. Paul was standing by the open door, staring into the night. After wresting a cup of instant coffee out of an ancient urn, Tom joined him there. 'How are you travelling?' he inquired.

'Knackered,' Paul said. 'Do you think they'd mind if I went to bed?'

'Just go for it. To tell you the truth, I was thinking of playing hooky myself for the remainder of the evening. I don't think I could sleep though, not quite yet. I feel like getting away from the constant surveillance. Just walk through the streets for a while by myself.'

'Good idea. Be careful though, won't you?'

'No worries. See you tomorrow.'

It was blissful for Tom walking in the dark, his skin colour, his difference, his otherworldliness momentarily forgotten. People passed him by in the poorly lit streets of the small town without so much as a nod, let alone the blunt stare he was becoming accustomed to.

His shoulders dropped and he exhaled. Walking for over an hour, he discovered a Philippines far less frenzied than before. Although there were still no road rules out here in the rural outskirts, there were far fewer vehicles at this time of night within the town — just a few motor scooters darting in and out of dirt alleyways leading from the parish hall. He found himself looking through windows of houses lit from within, and remembered he relished doing just this in his own street: a voyeur of sorts, glimpsing different lives from the safety of darkness, casting a lattice of invisibility over his own presence. Here, the scenes were similar, but more compact, less ambiguous: a mother and her young daughter propped on a wooden crate, belly-laughing at an American TV sitcom; two boys still in finely pressed school uniforms, heads bent down under the light of a kerosene lamp, doing what was probably the last of their homework for the day; and an aging man, the fingers of his right hand bent nearly at right angles, feeding an equally broken-down looking tabby cat.

Within these houses there was pain — that was obvious — but there was so much evidence of joy, of laughter, of love.

People were eating rice, washing with meagre amounts of water, relaxing where they had fallen against cardboard boxes, wooden pallets and other scattered belongings. Everything re-patched, rejuvenated, broken down again, recycled. Material reincarnation everywhere.

He struggled to understand, to frame the strangeness of what he saw. It was poverty, but multi-coloured — bright curtains framed by fractured concrete. Despite the age of things, the broken bones of the town, all had been cheerily painted in vivid colours, the dye of life; it was warm yellows and oranges, soothing greens and brilliant blues. It was also spotless. He wondered how the local people remained so neatly and cleanly attired. Even walking the muddy, unsealed roadways, their clothes seemed to remain untarnished. His trousers were already covered in clumps of red mud from the knees down and halos of sweat stained the underarms of his shirt.

A young woman crossed the road a few yards ahead of Tom. Her sinewy limbs moved with a focus that he had never witnessed before. He felt himself momentarily captivated, slightly envying her self-assured stance, the purpose that drove her stride and gaze. She signified to him a people concerned only with the road ahead of them. They seemed to ward off the grime of life simply with their manner, their attitude.

Tom walked back past the parish hall and peered inside. Everyone was sitting in the same positions, asking questions, shuffling papers, evidence was being given and collated. The faces within the hall looked far from tired. Instead, they flushed with the excitement of it all. He had seen animated faces such as these in Australia only at the football or at the horse races. Perhaps, Tom thought — endeavouring to glean something about this culture from the brief but intense tutorial he had received since arriving — vaudeville was not needed here. Life was the game. It was as open and real as their blushing faces.

I labour through meetings like it's a necessary evil, Tom thought, *but the people here look like they rejoice in their polity.*

Tom walked towards his sleeping quarters. In front of the building, leaning on a low-slung veranda, Maria stood smoking.

She'd wound a purple sarong around herself and her hair was down, falling in dark waves over her shoulders. She greeted him curtly. 'I wondered where you'd disappeared to. You missed some fascinating testimony.' Her tone was blunt, but completely genuine.

'I was busting for a walk. Needed some solitary time.'

Maria drew heavily on her cigarette and then scuffed it out with the sole of her sandal. She smiled warmly at him. 'Perhaps Westerners need more time alone than the rest of us.'

So perhaps she does have a sense of humour — when it suits her, thought Tom.

'I don't know about that,' he said 'We all need time to be alone, don't we?'

'Of course,' she said, 'but you need more time than we do. You are individuals at your core. We are a community.'

Her point reinforced his line of thinking. But he was too tired to take it further with her now. He smiled gently back at her. 'Goodnight, Maria. Sleep well.'

'You too, Thomas.'

After five minutes laying on a plywood platform without a mattress — known by the luxurious title of 'bed' — he was forced to the toilet by gripping pains in his stomach. As he fumbled with pieces of toilet paper he had stashed in his pack, he couldn't help but grin. Even on the toilet he was different. Most of the locals used their hands but he needed an instrument, an extra layer of separation and convenience. The husky voice of Maria came to him in his head, teasing: 'After all Thomas, you are still a capitalist at heart.'

4

HMC-Land

The trip from Bampakan to the mining headquarters took an hour. Along the way, a dramatic change took place: the rich forest had receded and the topsoil, bereft of its protective cover, had washed away into gullies and streams, gathering in great pits of silt at the bottoms of watercourses. Fists of naked rock jutted out to the exposed sky. *It's as if nothing exists upon this part of the Earth*, Tom thought.

'They must be the tailings dams,' he said to Father Ricardo, wedged in next to him in the driver's seat. Tom pointed to the earth and clay constructions set back from the road. 'They wouldn't pass first muster in the First World. The technology is primitive, barely scientific.'

He noticed a couple of families had burrowed in below the lip of the dam, creating some form of shelter with pieces of tin. He wondered if they knew how toxic their home was.

Ricardo kept his eyes on the road and remained silent.

Tom yelled a little louder. 'Father, the tailings dams are nothing more than mudpies thrown on top of each other — more evidence of environmental mismanagement. I bet they didn't even bother with an environmental impact assessment.'

Still, Ricardo stared straight ahead, no flicker of acknowledgement on his face. Tom turned his head to the back of the jeep and tried to catch Maria's eyes, but they too were engaged elsewhere. He wished Paul was here to make sense of things. He tried again, this time projecting his voice as loudly as he could. 'Father, the science of the whole operation has a lot to answer for — that meeting last night, I mean, the people in charge of the monitoring of the operations were not only biased, they were not even trained for such a task.'

At this point, Ricardo looked directly at him and then threw the jeep back into second gear, jerking the car off the road to a halt. He turned the engine off. 'Please desist with these arguments about environmental management and science. They will get you nowhere here. They are the arguments of the wealthy. Science has nothing to do with our struggle. The problem is simple: the transnational imperialists are taking our resources. They are ours, not theirs. We want them back. In good time, when the people are ready, we will mine the resources ourselves.'

'Yes Father, I understand. But can't you see that good environmental management will sustain the use of these precious resources? Have you heard of the concept of sustainability?'

At this point, Father Ricardo slammed his fist into the steering wheel. 'Dr McMahon. Yes, I know about *sustainability*. How could I not, when it dominates all the environmental management propaganda of the Company? It is capitalist-speak and once you enter their language you lose. It is they who win awards for sustainability. Not us.'

'Look, our objective today is simple: go to the HMC camp, shit in the flushing toilets and eat their very good rice,' Father Ricardo said. 'They get export-quality rice at the camp. And we must do it politely. Not asking rude questions.'

Tom got a little bit of a shock whenever the priest used profanities. But then he corrected himself: these sensibilities were his own, matching his First World impression of priestly stereotypes. Out here, it made sense — Ricardo was first and foremost a man of the people.

'Well then, what is the point?' he countered.

The priest sighed loudly. He turned on the ignition and swung the vehicle back onto the road.

Tom turned for some support from Maria, who smiled knowingly back at him. She moved close to his left ear and half whispered, 'The point, Thomas, is that in our media release we can say that the International Fact-Finding Mission consulted with the Company ... that we did not exclude their viewpoint. Understood?' She smiled again, flashing her white teeth. She sank back into her seat.

He wondered if Maria and the priest were gagging him. He wasn't sure he wanted *any* mining, whether it was HMC or the B'laan people themselves. Tom just thought it was the environmentally wrong thing to do.

Again, Ricardo's words to him after the basketball game echoed in his mind. Any real engagement with the Company could only lead to a loss of power, to the whittling away of solidarity and trust among the people. Defecating in the toilet, eating the free food — this was a deliberate position of disdain and non-engagement, the mock politeness further demonstrating that the activists' hearts were never really touched, never sullied by corporate greed.

At the boom gate, soldiers stood to attention, wearing the uniform of the Army and heavily laden with grenades and semi-automatic weapons. Tom noticed sentry boxes hanging on the fence high above the road, with heavy-calibre mounted machine guns aimed at their small jeep. As he peered upwards, he could make out similar boxes studding the periphery of the enclosure.

Inside the gate was a small man-made oasis, completely sovereign from the chaos of the surrounding landscape. Unnaturally green lawns sparkled under the relentless revolutions of sprinklers, bordered by gleaming stones painted in the Company colours of red, white and blue. In the middle of this vast lawn was a floral HMC logo. The now-familiar colour scheme glazed the prefabricated buildings of the camp, mimicking the architecture Tom had seen at Moomba Mines back in central Australia.

He remembered his last trip to Moomba. They had flown in at around midday. On hitting the tarmac, Tom and the other passengers had been led into a small, pristine waiting room within the airport, which was in a large, corrugated iron shed. Over its entry, a stylised blue, red and white sign read 'HMC'. After a cup of coffee, and a brief stretching of legs, they moved onto an air-conditioned bus. Over the next two hours, they ate sandwiches on the bus and toured Moomba Mines.

Despite the recent rains in the centre of Australia, Tom had observed little evidence of additional moisture at the mine site or around the township. Alongside the black macadam of the well-constructed roads lay a crimson dust, crushed from the rock that was the raison d'être of this human enterprise. This red ore had copper and uranium secreted inside it. The seemingly barren, obsolete landscape did have commercial *value* in it after all, but only beneath its surface. Caverns the size of entire cities were created beneath the earth, a complex system of roads and burrows dug tilting at forty-five degrees, so big that trucks five storeys high could hurtle unheeded towards their next payload.

The absolute *neatness* of the Moomba mine site struck Tom. Although HMC had ravaged the earth, they had done it under a veil of cleanliness and order. The only visible scars were cauterised entrance points for the vehicles and the miners. He had wrestled with the shape of the order, struggling to classify it, to describe it. *Is it military order?* No, this was more slick: less detritus, less visible waste. *This is corporate order*, he had decided.

This tautness, this prim regulation had been projected onto the township of Moomba as well. Tom searched for more details to articulate this feeling of starkness, this lack of life. There were no trees on the nature strips — that was one thing that easily stood out — only the single species of kikuyu grass. *The kind of grass that'll survive along with the cockroaches after Armageddon*, he had thought.

But it was the regularity of things, the exact repetition of measurements, a purity of angles that truly intrigued him. Mining engineers had built the town, not town planners, that was for sure. The entire municipality was a monoculture of design, each house a clone of the one next to it. And the place positively sparkled, as though someone had been employed to walk around with acid and a scrubbing brush to clean the curbs, the driveways, the façade. All of the buildings were painted in combinations of the HMC colours.

In Mindanao, here was HMC-land again, just as Disneyland had reinvented itself in Florida and then in Europe. *Perhaps a less virile clone*, Tom resolved. On his tour of Moomba, he remembered the Company receiving an award for a device that stopped yellow-bellied parrots landing on the tailings dams. In the Philippines, people took refuge in them.

Tom walked with Maria and the priest along a path of crunchy quartzite towards the reception building. They were accompanied by one of the security team who had jumped into their jeep at the entrance. Before they'd reached the door, Tom saw a familiar face beaming at him from the other side of the glass, in the building's foyer — Jenny Thompson, HMC's public relations manager, the same woman who had gasped with delight at the idea of 'green mining', the very one who had sent Patrick Walters off the deep end. *Same company, same people*, he thought. She leapt to the door, holding it open for the visitors.

'Dr McMahon,' she said. 'How wonderful to see you! And this must be the famous Father Ricardo. I've heard so much about you.'

She was dressed casually this time, in black slacks and a crisply pressed denim shirt. She wore the same vivid shade of lipstick as the last time Tom had seen her, as well as the same haughty expression.

Father Ricardo was quite taken aback by the welcome and looked decidedly uncomfortable. During Jenny Thompson's initial gasps of false wonderment she had totally ignored Maria, who was dressed simply, 'in solidarity with the community', as she had explained to Tom earlier that morning. She wore a blue cotton skirt and a white blouse, her thick hair bundled up under a scarf. Tom noticed that dark clouds had gathered quickly on Maria's face. He finally introduced her, feeling obliged to explain his previous acquaintance with Jenny Thompson. His initial shock at seeing Thompson quickly faded and he reminded himself again: same company, different place. No doubt Jenny Thompson had made the trip over to deal with just this situation, to provide the Company with intelligence on the Environment Centre and its president, and to deal firsthand with him.

Jenny locked arms with Tom as they walked down the hallway, squeezing his wrist. It was an attempt at recognition, a playful familiarity, a dash of flirtation, a symbol of oneness — *two Aussies over here together*. Her fingers touched his arm and he recoiled a little, hoping the priest or Maria didn't see this contact. But Maria glowered at the other woman. With no make-up and her hair swept away from her face, Maria's expression was more stark than usual, and her emotions seemed to be broadcast more clearly.

Jenny led them to a large office, seating the visitors. They were immediately introduced to the local PR manager, Dennis Reno. Polished, though possessing nowhere near the same levels of smoothness as Thompson, he spoke from a PowerPoint presentation on HMC's operations in Mindanao. Littered throughout the electronic slide show were the ubiquitous buzzwords Tom had heard before in his dealings with the Company: the 'triple-bottom line' of tight economic controls, environmental sustainability, social responsibility. Tom tried to make his face as expressionless as possible as he suffered through Reno's lecture on economics and rhetoric of globalisation. He'd heard it all before: how pursuing free-market economics would result in a 'trickle-down effect for the Philippines', creating more wealth for everyone, dispelling illiteracy, poverty and disease.

Reno spoke of the Australian Government's support for this 'aid project' that the Company was instigating, in the form of the new mine at nearby Mossy Mountain.

'And of course,' Reno added with a wave of his right hand, 'if we discover uranium alongside the copper ore, we can help save the planet from climate change. Our company in Australia is already doing this: cutting down our dependency on fossil fuels.'

He's hit all the bases, Tom thought. He remembered how much Patrick Walters had despised the way the mining lobby used the issue of climate change to promote pro-nuclear positions.

But in the half-hour presentation, there was no mention of the fact that the Company was actually involved in *mining*.

At the end, Jenny Thompson said, 'Why, thank you Denis for your most informative presentation. I certainly learnt a lot about operations here. Now, what we've got planned is a lovely lunch … a chance to meet some of the rest of our management team here, as well as some of the local dignitaries with whom we work so closely. Then, if time permits, perhaps a tour of our operations here?'

Questions from the floor had not been scheduled. Tom was conscious of Father Ricardo's request for him to be polite but he just couldn't let Jenny Thompson escape that easily.

'Excuse me Jenny,' he said, 'is there going to be any opportunity to ask questions? There are a couple of issues that I would like to raise.'

Jenny Thompson knew his game well. She glanced at her watch and then to Reno, who rather innocently said, 'Of course, Dr McMahon, I would be delighted to address any issue you wish to raise.'

'You're most generous. Your presentation did provide much information about your current operations at the broadbrush level. As you are probably aware, I'm particularly interested in the environmental management side of the process.' He fleetingly looked at Father Ricardo for any signs of annoyance. There were none, though he saw that Maria had started squirming in her seat. 'I noticed the tailings dams on the way in. Exactly what kind of treatment processes are being used here?'

'I'm afraid I haven't got the sort of scientific training to address these tintack issues, Dr McMahon. I'm more of a big picture man, myself. But I do know they exceed local government minimum standards by some substantial extent,' Reno said. He then bent down, picked up a stack of bound folders and unloaded several heavy volumes of reports in front of Tom as evidence of HMC's commitment to good ecological governance.

While Reno droned on, Tom flicked through a report produced by the Company for the newly proposed mine at Mossy Mountain. Tom was amazed to learn that the problems of tailings dams would be largely bypassed in the new mine, as he read that 'marine disposal' was HMC's preferred choice. This form of tailings disposal would destroy fishing grounds for hundreds of kilometres along the coast. He almost blurted out his opposition but, conscious of the priest's request, he counted to ten, and then at the next available opportunity said, 'Thanks for this report, Mr Reno. It really is most informative.'

'Thank you Dr McMahon. It is a draft report only, I must add, and is not fit for public consumption at the moment.'

Conversation petered out and Jenny asked if everyone was ready for lunch. Quietly, Tom put the draft report into his leather satchel and shuffled towards the banquet room.

The priest was right. The rice was good and after lunch Tom relaxed on the flushing toilet. There was even toilet paper, provided by a bowl-side dispenser.

As Jenny escorted them to the jeep, the hot sun deflected painful shards of white light off the gravel. High up on Mossy Mountain, its twin peaks engulfed in a gentle mist, a Philippines Eagle sailed on the updraft in ever-increasing circles. Just short of the jeep, Jenny Thompson grabbed Tom by the seam of his pants with her thumb and forefinger. Tom noticed Maria's nostrils flare from the back seat. He tried to meet her eye but she was now busying herself with her tape recorder.

'Tom. Please don't take any offence if the guards at the gate check your bag. Just standard procedure,' Jenny said, staring straight into his eyes. 'We would hate to have any official documentation fall into the wrong hands.'

'Of course not, Jenny,' he said.

Then he jumped into the back of the jeep, leaving the priest slightly perplexed on his own in the front. He sat down and opened his bag, then shoved the bulky report under Maria's backside. As the whites of her eyes flashed with surprise, he motioned for her to be silent, moving his index finger to his lips. When they reached the gate, the phone rang inside the main sentry box. The guards were most apologetic when they asked him to open his bag. They found nothing and then, just as they were contemplating searching the rest of the jeep's occupants, the priest muttered something to them in the local dialect, waving his hand at the boom gate, insisting that they open it without further delays. Whatever he said did the trick.

As they sped along the road, Maria smiled at Tom. 'Fruits of battle?'

'Sorry to be so presumptuous. But it was the only way.'

'Not at all. Anything for a good cause. What is it, anyway?'

'The draft EIA report for Mossy Mountain. Thought we could use it in the IFFM's press release. If you don't want to use the information over here then that's fine, but I can use it at home to hit the Company where its shareholders are.'

She smiled and lowered her voice: 'Later, we can go over it together

… before we show it to Father. Okay?'

Tom looked at her gratefully. Their eyes held.

* * *

Back at the compound, for the rest of the afternoon Tom managed to sneak away into the room he shared with the youngest curate, Peter. For the first time in days he managed to fall into a profound sleep.

Dad had him again.

He'd bribed Tom with Minties, raspberry lemonade and chips. Sitting at the bar, talking in a gruff voice to his mates, he was a big man, big and blond. Dad laughed with these strange people, all red-faced men, all smelling the same way. Tom liked the way he smiled — he didn't do it very often.

The nights were awful. They slept in a caravan, backing onto a cliff above the sea. Sean stewed in his own shit — his cloth nappy rarely got changed. After the orphanage, Tom had to sleep with Dad, who got angry when Tom couldn't get his own jodhpurs off. He'd roll from side to side in bed, pushing Tom out. Tom would walk around to the other side but then Dad rolled that way too.

Now, in the first touches of evening, he woke feeling strangely refreshed — despite his disturbing dreams — and in high spirits. He decided to wash and change his shirt. There was some fresh fruit on the table so he grabbed a pawpaw, dug out his pocket knife and sat at the curate's desk, peering out the window. The fruit was so juicy that it quenched his thirst and knocked the edge off his hunger. He was halfway through his second piece of fruit when there was a knock at the door. It was Maria. Tom noticed she was freshly showered, her wet hair even blacker than usual and slicked back from her moist temples, like a cap. He liked how he could see her face more this way, though he thought this made her look vulnerable, almost childlike. She was also dressed strangely, in camouflaged military fatigues.

'Thomas, I've drafted the piece for our media release. Sorry, it couldn't wait. It's in the jeep. You can read it on the way.'

'On the way?'

'Yes, I have a little surprise for you.'

As he followed her into the jeep he was rather disappointed to see Paul sitting in the back seat. His realisation that he wanted to be alone with Maria jolted him. He managed a smile.

'Paul, how are you, my friend? What have you been up to?' he asked as he climbed in next to him.

'I had a very interesting time today visiting an HMC-funded school. You would have loved it, Thomas. The children were singing the Company song. They had HMC everything: rulers, notepads and pencils … even comic books, with HMC's version of Ronald McDonald.'

'What the hell would such a creature look like?'

'He's … I think he is a … he's a type of beaver or gopher, but bigger. A small bear, even. Some sort of furry, digging creature anyway, with a hard hat and a shovel.'

'Not a wombat?'

'That's it! Wally the Wombat. He's dressed in blue overalls with the HMC logo on his front pocket. He's very hard-working, honest and concerned for everyone. He's Mickey Mouse but — how shall I put it — Mickey Mouse with a penchant for mining. Or even better, for liberating the poor minerals trapped underneath the oppression of the earth's surface!'

As the men shared a dark laugh, Maria was fussing about busily under the bonnet of the jeep, looking very capable despite the fact that a string of profanities flew out from beneath it. Tom knew nothing of mechanics. He would have loved to be able to help, to look like a man in command, but she slammed down the bonnet, her hands and part of her face covered in grease. She spat out sentences in Filipino and Spanish.

'Fucking jeep,' she said finally. 'I've told Father that it is no good anymore.' She revved the engine until bursting point, perhaps as some kind of punishment for the filth it had just inflicted upon her, and then ground it into first, letting the clutch fly.

This time there was no sealed road, and just when Tom thought that they could get no further into the jungle, Maria found some other skerrick of roadway — too faint even to be called a track — and then it seemed they were on no track at all again. The jeep moved slowly through the undergrowth of a thick rainforest, lantana vines threatening to drag them out of the car. But Maria looked totally unfazed. She was following some map in her mind, reaching for some predetermined destination. For an hour they travelled like this, moving deeper into the forest, the evening cry of cicadas so loud they began to rise above the unremitting whine of the jeep.

Finally they came to a standstill and Maria sprang out of the vehicle, not even bothering with the door.

'Grab the water bottle and the pack in the back,' she told Paul. She came around to Tom's side of the vehicle and looked at his feet. 'Shit,' she hissed. 'You're still fucking dressed from the Company visit. We've got quite a way to go yet.'

Tom glanced up at Paul. Somehow the lawyer had known more about the purpose of this rather spontaneous field trip, as he was wearing hiking boots and gaiters.

'I'm sorry Maria, but I was actually dressed for dinner, not for trekking,' Tom said. 'If you'd mentioned before, I could have—'

'It doesn't matter. If you get wet, just take your shoes off when we get back to the car. On second thoughts, take them off now. Barefoot would be better. We can burn the leeches off with matches later.'

'Gee, thanks,' Tom mumbled, smiling warily.

Before he'd tucked his shoes and socks away in the jeep, she barked more orders to hurry up, some of her earlier surliness returning. 'Quickly Thomas, or it will be too dark to find our way.'

What little moonlight that found its way down to them infused a ghostly, mottled glow across the forest floor. She came back to him and took his hand. 'Just ... be careful. Follow my footsteps.'

Careful of what? Tom wondered, struck by a pinprick of fear.

Tom's anxieties dispersed temporarily as he felt the first squish of sodden humus through his toes. At first he found it a little repulsive, but with each moment of contact it became increasingly liberating. As the trek continued, he felt a sensation strengthened by the firm grip of Maria's hand.

Still further they pushed into the forest. He tried to catch a glimpse of the apex of the trees. But even if he had been lying flat on his back this goal would be unattainable. Mahogany trees soared to heights unimaginable, their thick trunks punching through high cloud.

He sensed no wind within the forest. Without any movement of air, each sound reverberated as if it existed within an enormous drum. Beyond the harping of cicadas, beyond the bass drone of the mosquitoes, voices, human voices, became more audible. Tom looked around and glanced up at the trees.

'Maria, Paul ... can you hear that?'

'Don't worry. They're expecting us,' Maria said.

'Who?'

'I said don't worry.'

In spite of Maria's assurances, fear began to stir deep inside Tom's belly. Shadows shifted in the forest, vegetation shuffled in the corner of his eye. Unsure if it was his own anxiety — his own lack of control — producing only tricks of the light, or whether these events existed in real time and space, Tom's senses heightened, his body tingling.

There. He was sure he'd seen something. Eyes. A face. And then he witnessed two bodies scurrying from his left, out of his line of sight. Touching Maria on the arm, he gestured to a man sitting high in the limbs of a tree, a gun pointed directly at his face. She nodded, held her index finger to her lips and waved him on.

In the last one hundred metres of their journey, the forest floor formed a natural meadow, though the canopy still provided an impenetrable dome. In this more open terrain, Tom noticed a thick mist swelling across the forest floor, the result of the last heat of the day escaping from the earth before the full onset of the cooler night.

Amidst the haze loomed a group of men in guerrilla fatigues, communicating in hushed voices.

Tom and Paul froze on the spot. Maria again gestured for them to follow her. 'I already told you — don't stress, they know we're here.'

Most of the troops involved themselves in unarmed combat exercises and seemed unperturbed by the interlopers. But it was a bit like watching someone practice the tuba with no mouthpiece. Mute violence. Tom turned to Maria for explanation, but she was busily threading them through the crowded meadow. Finally, two armed guards forced them to a halt. Maria produced some documentation, immediately putting the guards at ease. The guards led them through a mass of soldiers — Tom guessed two or three hundred — to a series of small tents on the edge of the natural parade ground. Again, guards asked them to produce their papers. After five minutes or so, out of one of the tents walked a man who, when he clapped eyes on Maria, broke into an ear-splitting grin.

'Sergeant Cortes,' he said, as he moved to embrace her. They spoke animatedly for a good minute, before he looked at the two men she had brought with her.

Maria took over the introductions. 'Dr McMahon, from Australia, and Mr Paul Benguet, our legal aid from Manila. This is Colonel Sichon, Commander of the 24th Regiment of the People's Liberation Army … what is called the Green Army.'

The colonel was a fine-featured man. He was wiry, with a light moustache and a full head of thick hair. Around his eyes were the etchings of a man who was fully present in the moment and smiled often. Tom observed the lack of any discerning signs of rank on his battle fatigues. Something about him said 'poet' more than 'militiaman', Tom reflected.

'A pleasure to meet you, Colonel,' Tom said.

'As it is you, comrade. We are fully supportive of your International Fact-Finding Mission and feel it very necessary to get the people's plight known outside of this island.'

Tom had the feeling that the colonel was regurgitating a prepared response, similar to the briefing that Enrico had given on Tom's very first day in the Philippines. Again, his English seemed too impeccable, impossibly out-of-place here, deep within this rainforest.

Colonel Sichon gestured to his regiment with an extended arm. 'These men and women have been stationed in this area in direct response to the threat which Horizon Mining Corporation poses for our people. We are securing the area around Mossy Mountain for your visit there in the next few days. It is important that the people know of your arrival and your good purpose. It is rare that foreigners are here for purposes other than exploitation. But I have already said enough. I must return to my work. Please feel free to move around the regiment. You are in very capable hands; I would trust Sergeant Cortes with my life.'

He shook their hands again and disappeared into his tent.

Maria gestured to them to take a seat on a tarpaulin spread on the ground. Her intensity had waned.

'Have you ever seen anything like this, gentlemen?' she said, smiling and fishing for reactions. But before they could answer, she spoke to Tom: 'This is what we mean by mass mobilisation. You see, not just bringing people together for a day-long rally or peace march. We are at war with the Company. I brought you here because I couldn't see any other way of explaining it.'

To Tom, non-violent action was a non-negotiable position, a benchmark for all the green activists he knew back in Australia. From the radical edge occupied by the Patrick Walters of the world, to the corporate pragmatism of Louise at the other end of the spectrum, this had always been one point where everyone had agreed. Once again, Tom felt his political worldview — his ideological bricks-and-mortar — being hit with a battering ram.

As if reading his mind, Maria spoke directly to him.

'Non-violence is a luxury position of the West,' she retorted. 'The people on Mossy Mountain have no negotiating power. Non-violent resistance would mean either death or displacement.'

Tom looked at Paul for some support but his friend did not interject. All he could now do was spout a cliché, a one-liner which he'd previously understood as an untouchable kernel of sacred truth. 'But the ends can never justify the means,' Tom persisted.

'Look, Thomas. I am not going to argue with you. We have no Gandhi here. There is no such tradition.'

'But do the priests … does the Church know about this armed resistance?'

'Some do, some don't. Most turn a blind eye. But you're right, it is a source of some tension. After Marcos was ousted, we put faith in representative democracy. We supported Aquino. Then the military turned on our people anyway. It was then that I joined the Liberation Army.'

'But you're a journalist. And you've got journalistic ethics …

surely? How can you be a sergeant in the PLA and still cover the story objectively?"

Maria sat silently for a moment. She wrestled with some unruly strands of hair that had come loose from under her cap.

'There is no place for fence-sitters in the Philippines,' she said. 'Fence-sitting means death. You must decide which side you are on.'

He knew now that Maria was not directing any malice at him. His sense was that she harboured a deep-seated anger and it vented itself against all those who squeezed life's juices out of her people.

Suddenly they heard a beating noise in the distance, from the sky, moving closer to the amphitheatre. Without an order, the regiment dispersed. The tents were down in a single moment and Maria grabbed the two men by the arms, running to get cover within the thicker part of the forest. Tom looked up but already the Green Army was gone, as if swallowed by the forest.

'Choppers. American choppers on loan to the National Army,' Maria said. 'They are looking for us — the Regiment. To them we are just bandits, terrorists.'

Tom's heart began to thrum. Sensing his fear, Maria grabbed his hand and made firm eye contact.

'Don't worry,' she said. 'They will not find us. The canopy is too perfect. That is why the first thing the government does is sell off the forest. Not for the wood, but to destroy our vantage points, our hiding places.'

Still, she held her head low as the helicopters hovered above them, their screaming engines shattering the forest's tranquillity. For some minutes, Tom felt certain that the persistent hovering of the choppers would strip the vegetation off the massive branches that bore the weight of the forest's ceiling. The violent down-draughts threw birds from their nests in every direction. Insects and other forest debris lodged in

Tom's mouth, his nostrils, making it almost impossible to breathe. He clutched at the earth beneath him, too scared to move. He felt as if he was drowning in the forest. He remembered again the blackness of the river.

And the blackness of the night as a child.

His father never let him sleep with the light on. How could he explain to his dad that the night-light was a candle Mum had lit for Tom and Sean in heaven? With the curtains drawn down against his enemies, perceived or real, Tom's father created a complete darkness that made everything else void. When his darling mother was still alive — although her mind and body were broken in a hospital bed — Tom had some base-point, some port-of-call in the great scheme of things. But now, since she had taken her own life, Tom — weightless in an adult world — sensed himself shrinking against the unpredictability of the violent force that was his father, lying next to him.

Mummy ... why did you go?

Just a feather of self left.

* * *

After some minutes, Tom at last sensed that the wind howling through his ears was diminishing. And then they were gone. The gunships, like giant hands stretched across the moon, began to move to another point on their search-and-destroy mission. As they retreated, Maria shouted over the remaining din, 'And they would be too scared to come in here at ground level. We would skin them alive.'

Tom knew that she meant it.

5

Dawn Service

A full hour before dawn, the parish compound was already bustling. Tom's bedroom backed onto the mudbrick wall of the kitchen and the clattering pots and pans woke him. He listened intently to the sounds of morning in Bampakan: the dragging in of wood and the lighting of fires, earthen floors being scratched clean with stick brooms. Out of respect for the priests — who seemed to be up late at meetings every night — the cooks kept their voices to a gentle murmur.

A tapping at the door revealed a wizened elderly man who whispered something to Peter, the young priest and Tom's room-mate, in a bid to wake him. The old man delivered a large pitcher of warm water and then retreated. As soon as he departed, the curate threw back the sheets, his feet hitting the floor with a thump. He crept about the room, performing his basic ablutions and then changed into his vestry garments. Tom watched as he plastered his black, wavy hair down with old-style hair cream and imposed a strict part on the left side of his head, a style Tom remembered from his childhood. The young priest moved to a desk under a small window and began to read.

After a time, he looked up from his preparations and saw that his visitor was watching him.

'Good morning,' he said, in what Tom thought was an overly cheery manner for this hour of the day. 'Are you coming to mass, Dr McMahon?'

Tom looked at the curate blankly. Nothing could have been

further from his mind. But the curate added, with an excitement barely containable, 'Father Jose … he asked me to do the mass this morning … his meeting didn't end until three.'

His eyes darted back to his notes. An ornate copy of the Bible sat in front of him on top of his simple desk, and he studied it for ten minutes more before he spoke again. 'I'm going to give a mass in your honour, the International Fact-Finding Mission's honour. The whole town is happy with the news of your Mission.'

Finally managing to get to a point where speech was possible, he mumbled, 'Good morning Peter. Yes … I'd be honoured to come to your mass.'

Leaping from his chair, Peter poured water into a tin basin from the large jug and motioned for Tom to wash himself. A big grin broke out on Peter's face. 'The kitchen is making big breakfast. After mass we eat like the apostles!'

I hope it's not the last supper, thought Tom.

'See you later, Dr McMahon. You can make your own way? Mass in fifteen minutes.'

The curate disappeared through the door, to Tom a bundle of hope and energy. Tom caught sight of himself in a broken shard of mirror that Peter had shaved in front of minutes earlier.

'Bloody idiot,' he mumbled, as he remembered again that he'd only packed his electric razor and, as a result, hadn't shaved for nearly a week. He liked to be a model of regularity when it came to 'scraping his face', as he called it, so the thick black stubble sprinkled with grey around his chin felt alien to his touch. Not in the habit of staring at himself in the mirror, the sight of his own reflection gave him a bit of a jolt: dark rings had formed around washed-out eyes, their once fierce blue now the colour of cornflower. The sprouting beard defined the edges of his face with a severe clarity, hollowing flesh and pronouncing the ridges of his cheekbones.

'I look knackered,' he said out loud.

As soon as he washed and dressed, Tom took a plastic bag of used socks and underwear out of his case and rinsed them in the bowl of used water. After wringing them out, he perched them on a towel on the floor, trying to catch a moving square of sunlight from the window. He then re-ordered his suitcase and felt a little bit more in control.

Tom moved to the veranda that joined all of the rooms to a central courtyard. The air was fresh and moist, and for the first time since arriving in the Philippines he felt a slight shiver. The goosebumps on his arms reminded him that he was now in the foothills of a mountain range, already some hundreds of metres above sea level.

In the middle of the yard stood a huge fig tree, its brawny roots stretching out to all corners of the quadrangle. Its broad leaves of deep green caught the stripes of dawn still hovering in the sky, turning them into leafy cups of liquid purple.

He walked towards the construction site of the new church. Three walls and the roof were already up and, as if by design, the incomplete wall was on the eastern side, providing the congregation with front row seats to watch the continued unveiling of the morning sun. The new church could seat five hundred people and even at this early hour, on a Wednesday morning, it was three-quarters full.

The congregation crammed the hall, people still with sleep on their faces. Some had impressions of their bedding stamped onto their skin. This was an everyday place, not just a location for special occasions — simply the beginning of the day for the locals of Bampakan. Men, women, babies, the very elderly — all of them awoke gently in this space of communion and community, quietly whispering well-trodden responses to the priest's prayers.

Tom felt strangely comfortable, though he hadn't been to mass for years. The Filipino language of the service washed over him; there were no words of meaning to distract him. But the metre and rhythm of the words and phrases were familiar — a hypnotic drumbeat from his childhood.

The recent mosquito coil conversation on the roadside with Paul tugged at him. And then there were the daydreams of his father: remembrances of past fishing trips, and a mixture of troubled and jumbled images from his youth that he'd long buried. His inner knowing — if not his conscious mind — pointed him along one pathway, in the direction of the suffering. He fought off the thoughts again. 'Self-indulgent bullshit,' he muttered under his breath. But he moved against his standard response and tried once more. He had always hated bullies, had always despised the inappropriate use of power. Sitting on a pew in a half-built church in Mindanao, Tom searched for the earliest memories of oppression in his own life, this feeling of an outer force that he fought against; a dangerous force, a force much more powerful than himself. His discomfort, his exhaustion, the assault on every one of his senses since he had arrived in the Philippines, had altered his thought pathways. He floated away, beyond his tightly held reason. He drifted to where his memories had begun.

He'd been in his cot. His eyes had opened and he knew he was alive. The first sensation he felt was thirst. He cried into the darkness. He wailed, and a much deeper wail came from the other room. It belonged to that big creature, the angry one. The softer creature entered the room with a container of colourless liquid in her hand. Already he had felt it: love. With the container held to his mouth, he immediately tasted the coolness, the silkiness of the liquid wet upon his lips, then the roof of his tongue and mouth, and then the back of his throat. The ache deep in his neck had ceased. One container was not enough, but he could not communicate this.

Previously, he had no desire to unravel the tightly wound ball of his childhood experience, or his memories. It was just him, who he was. But now his thoughts slid into an underworld where there were no rules of engagement.

He shuffled uncomfortably on the pew. Thoughts he had let lie for so long trickled and bubbled to the surface. The digging up of such deep and rancid matter from the hidden gardens of his psyche was exhausting. When the time came for the congregation to move onto their knees to pray, he did so with gratitude, shielding his tears, his hands draped over his face. Between the unknown words came the familiar 'Amen', which he seized upon as a constant, droning pulse, enabling him to move back into the world around him.

The congregation sat down again. He took a deep breath. Although he housed a deep pain, he had not let it destroy him. His whole life he had fed directly upon its poison and, in a remarkable act of will, he had converted the detritus into an inner strength, rooted in pain and made durable, hardened by hate. But Tom already knew that this type of strength comes at a terrible cost. Born of an oath of self-reliance, a vow to trust no-one else but oneself, its potency was double-edged.

He cleared his tears — strange, sparkling jewels he never thought he'd experience again — and set his jaw once more. What mattered, he decided, was that he could still see the beauty in people and the world moving around and beyond them.

He was so tired he couldn't imagine how he would get through the day ahead. The land of the power nap was non-existent where he was. His mind no longer behaved in its usually disciplined manner. His social science training was lost in an exotic novel, a story without proof or repeatability. The tight order of life he had fought for was fizzing and unravelling.

He noticed the priest now talking in English. His own native tongue snapped Tom from his stupor.

'I have spoken today of the International Fact-Finding Mission and its important undertaking … a mission to question the facts about HMC's mining operations here in Bampakan. And I want to thank Dr Thomas McMahon, sitting in our congregation today. We wish Dr McMahon, and his friends, every blessing.'

The young curate then spoke in the local dialect, and with these words he smiled broadly, gesturing to the back of the church where Tom sat. The congregation turned and faced him. Some beamed in a smile as broad as the priest's. Others looked quizzically at him, as if they'd been given a good excuse to stare at the stranger. But all of the gazes were open to him. No more words were needed. He felt a huge swelling in his chest, an energy directed towards him, and it felt as if the very marrow of his bones was beginning to warm and tingle.

The priest slid back into ritual mode, making preparations for the taking of the sacrament. Again the language moved beyond Tom's own understanding, but the movements of the priest were regular and universal. The sun was beginning to climb now and for a brief moment, just before it disappeared above the low roofline, its rays intensified. The congregation moved to the aisles, heads hung in preparation for taking the Eucharist.

Tom didn't know whether he should take it or not. Part of him wanted to, but then his cold reason took hold again: surely it would be wrong to be involved in a sacred ritual that he'd been taught to revere so much as a child?

At the end of the service, people moved towards him. An old man with stories of pain welling in his dark eyes looked into him, shook his hands warmly and thanked him for his presence. Young mothers, practising their broken English, introduced their children to him, proudly boasting of the achievements of their offspring. Others touched him with reverence, while others laughed with him.

The young priest gently broke up the small crowd still lingering around Tom. He took Tom's arm and walked with him back into the confines of the presbytery, where the promised sumptuous breakfast stood waiting. When they entered the earthen-floored kitchen, a vast table strained under a huge weight of foods: fried fish with their heads still intact; boiled chickens, rabbits and other game; a plate stacked high with assorted offal; and a mountain of steamed rice. In rural Mindanao, there seemed to be no difference between breakfast, lunch or dinner fare.

The members of the Fact-Finding Mission, the priests and local dignitaries surrounded the food. No sooner did Tom and Peter enter the room than Maria stood up, gesturing for him to sit down at a seat between Father Ricardo and herself. When he took his place, she smiled and began preparing a plate of food for him. The parish priest, even though he had missed mass, must have known of Tom's early morning churchgoing, catching him unawares when he asked him to say grace. Although rather flustered at first, the words of prayer came back to him.

In fact, so confident was he of his performance that at the end of the stock, everyday verse he added, 'And apart from thanking God for this grand meal, on behalf of the Fact-Finding Mission I wish to thank the parish and people of Bampakan for their generosity of spirit — the wonderful welcome they have extended to us.'

With this off-the-cuff addition, the parish priest nodded in silent approval and muttered, 'Amen,' for the second time.

'You have done very well, Thomas. Now you have the clergy on your side,' Maria said quietly, after several mouthfuls of food. She beamed, her head bent over her bowl.

Before he could respond, he felt a tap on his right arm from Father Ricardo. 'You went to the mass?' he enquired.

'Yes. It was wonderful, Father. Peter did an excellent job. Dedicated the mass to our Mission. The support of the people was just great. In Australia, the Church lacks that kind of vitality, I reckon.'

'You are right, my friend. I have visited my Australian brethren and understand some of their problems. But here the Church has its own axe to grind as well. Be sure of that. The Church is a significant part of the network of resistance, but sometimes it makes the mistake of thinking that it is the most important part. The Muslim community is just as necessary. And so are those who seek no spiritual guidance.'

Strange yet honest words from a Catholic priest, he thought.

Tom took another mouthful. He was beginning to like eating rice with his hand.

'I like the way the Church is connected to people's lives,' he said. 'The way it faces the issues of the present, not just prattling on about rewards in the afterlife.'

'Yes, you make an interesting point,' Ricardo said. 'But you must appreciate that not all Christian churches play such a role. In the last decade we have seen a large increase in the number of American evangelical churches in Mindanao. They sell their version of heaven to the poorest of our peasants, preaching patience … subservience to the wealthy. These are the Churches of slavery, the Churches of capitalism.'

When Tom's plate was half empty, Maria moved about him and made sure it overflowed again. He felt in her good books now, though he was at a bit of a loss as to how he had made this transition from archenemy to archangel. But he didn't complain. He already knew that she could be a formidable foe. Now, perhaps, she would turn out to be a formidable friend.

He watched her hands as she served from each dish onto his plate. *Wonderful hands*, he thought. They were slender, each finger a work of the most exquisite design. A simple ring of silver sat on the middle finger of her right hand, but he did not know if this signified anything about her marital status or not. The elegance of the ring heightened his appreciation for her natural beauty, captured before him in the dance of her hands. There was a sting of sensuality about them, coupled with a strong sense of capability: the nails were cut neat and short, and her fingers moved boldly through space. Although his conversation was engaged with Ricardo, Tom's body was sharing space with Maria. An electricity sparked between them, raw and strong.

As soon as Tom had finished his second plate, Paul tapped him on the shoulder. 'Got a minute?' he said, motioning him away from the table.

There were so many conversations at the table — so much noise — that it was unnecessary to excuse himself. Maria, in an ardent exchange with another woman seated across from her, acknowledged his departure by touching him on the wrist, although she continued with her discussion. Tom saw Paul register the brief contact as they moved out of the kitchen altogether.

'Sorry for interrupting,' Paul said as they walked through the quadrangle. 'I just wanted to catch up with you before we disappear on our separate errands. After yesterday, who knows where we're headed!' Paul played again with his small beard, separating each strand in a repetitive sequence known only to him. His eyes glinted with mischief. 'I wanted to tell you that she asked me this morning whether you were *attached*. I did mention that you were married, but she didn't seem to flinch at that.'

Tom blushed but then denied what he had already felt. 'Who are you talking about?'

For some reason he took slights from Paul he would not tolerate from others. Paul was a strange combination for him: part of both worlds, Australia and the Philippines. This combination of familiarity and otherness — as well as his dry sense of humour — seemed to give Paul a pass into places not permitted to others.

'Ms Cortes.'

Tom shuffled uncomfortably, making a snap decision to change the subject. 'Did you get some rest last night?'

Paul let him go this time. 'Well, I think four or five hours is considered indulgence down here. So yes, far better than the previous nights. What about you?'

'Yeah, alright. I went for a walk and that settled me down a bit. But I was up at dawn in time for mass.'

'Mass?' said Paul in mock astonishment. 'What did you want to do that for? That's right, you're one of us. I remember now. To atone for future sins you plan embarking upon with Ms Cortes?' he laughed.

'It's a long story. Got hooked into it. But I've got to say, it was a rather remarkable experience. Got me thinking about our conversation the other night.'

Paul was in an effusively cheerful mood. Some decent sleep and a belly full of good food suited him. 'Geez, Tom. If you don't mind me saying, you've got me a bit worried. First I discover you're a chick magnet. And now you're a new age sensitive guy!'

But Tom remained serious. 'Yes, I know. I've been thinking strangely. About things I thought dead and buried. And I've had a few really weird dreams. I feel like I'm losing it a bit.'

'About Maria,' Paul said, but then he noticed the full depth of Tom's mood. 'Look Tom, it's nothing to worry about. It's probably just that you're out of your routine. Listen, I just remembered what I really wanted to talk to you about. I've found an ISD booth, not far from here. I was looking for some handicrafts to take back to Manila with me, you know, for presents. Why don't you ring home? That'll straighten you up.'

Tom knew he had been delaying making the inevitable phone call since his arrival and the paucity of opportunities to ring home had provided some justification, but not all.

Since having children, the only occasions when Tom and Amanda really spoke during the week was on the phone from work. By telephone they discussed the children, wrestled with the familial finances and planned upcoming weekend adventures. Even then, they blocked the phone calls in between other tasks, other obligations. On days such as these, after weeks such as these, Tom felt his marriage move slightly at its base. He knew he had to make more time for Amanda, his partner and confidante, but he struggled to comprehend how he could achieve this.

In Melbourne, on the night before his departure, Tom had noticed how tired, how world-weary she looked. But he knew that her vital spirit had not been broken. Grey shadows under her grey eyes only accentuated her silver beauty and the first flecks of it in her hair highlighted the quality of her complexion. She carried herself with pride; she had always moved in a way that he'd thought of as regal.

He wanted to hold her now, to be held by her. He wanted the familiarity of the past to float in their sea of shared moments and he yearned to tell her how beautiful she was. He wanted to tell her of his discoveries. His passion for the world around him had once burned for her as well.

Tom found the phone booth easily, about half a kilometre from the compound gates in a small cluster of shops. He dialled the long string of numbers.

'Hello … Amanda Robinson,' came the answer.

'Amanda, it's me,' he spluttered, almost in tears again.

She sensed the difference immediately. 'Are you alright, Tom?'

'Oh, yep. I'm just a bit exhausted, that's all. Are you alright? The kids alright?'

There was a distance between them before he left and it had clearly grown since his departure. Amanda's initial concern was replaced with a hardness, a coldness. 'So you're actually interested in your family now, are you?'

'What's that supposed to mean?'

'Well, the children have been constantly asking after you and we haven't heard from you in nearly a week. I didn't even know if you'd arrived safely!'

'I told you it might be hard to phone.'

'Oh bullshit, Tom. You're off saving the bloody world again. Only, we don't get a look-in. And you know I've *got* to get to the Chaucer conference in London in a fortnight. Barely been able to scratch a couple of minutes together to write the paper. You know how important this paper is for the promotion. I can hardly ask Mother to look after the kids any more than I already have. She's got her own work to do.'

The conversation continued in a disastrous way. Perhaps that's why he'd been putting it off. Amanda was still fuming at him for going, for putting himself in the line of fire; for risking his life unnecessarily.

'Look, Amanda. It's perfectly safe here. I'm in the best hands possible. Don't believe what you see on telly — I haven't even seen my first terrorist yet!' he said, trying to lighten the mood.

'Yes. Well it's good that *you* think you're safe,' she said, sounding unconvinced.

'Are the kids alright?'

'Yes. Nothing abnormal to report. Emily's had a bit of a virus. Nothing major.'

'Can you give them a kiss from me?'

'No. Phone kisses aren't good enough. Wait until you're home — then you can do it yourself.'

This last dart fed on his recent revelations, his newly released memories. He had planned to debrief a little with Amanda, to share his fears, his feelings. On some level, he knew he could hardly expect the sympathetic ear that he needed. So he pretended to ignore her last comment, deciding to cut the conversation short. 'Well, I'll try ringing again when I'm back in General Santos City, in about three or four days' time.'

'Alright, Tom. But only if it doesn't interfere with your plans to bring peace to Mindanao.'

As he walked unsteadily back from the phone booth to the compound, dodging the onslaught of jeepneys, motor scooters and donkey-carts, another flash from the past came to him.

He had his head on his mother's lap. She had just put in eardrops to relieve a blackness of pain that had stricken him. She stroked his temples and gently tugged on his earlobes, working the heated liquid deeper into his ear canal. She whispered to him gently, willing the wax to break up, to dislodge the blockage.

'I think it's working, darling. Well done. You'll be feeling better in no time,' she said.

Her smell. Her softness. Her kindness. Back in a time when the family still existed, before her final plummet into the madness that had talked her own hand into snuffing out her life. Lost forever.

Lying down under the huge fig tree in the compound quadrangle, he closed his eyes. This was how the Philippines made him feel: like clumps of matter breaking free from the stem of his brain, floating upwards into the light of day. But any thoughts of his mother — whatever few he could remember — always led him back to Dad, however much he resisted it.

Around and around the kitchen they went. Like a dog chasing a hare. Dad was wielding a knife. Mum was screaming. Tom was in his cowboy outfit. Santa had given it to him for being a good boy. He was happy because it was new. Why weren't they happy?

He recalled sitting in the kitchen. It was dusk. The smell of the pine Christmas tree wafted down the hallway. Dad was somewhere on the threshold, arriving home. Mum was desperately trying to get Tom and Sean off to bed. But it was too late. Two small children — Sean a toddler and Tom only three-and-a-half — caught in the maelstrom. Dad threw them from their bunks, against the walls.

Tom had learnt to roll into a ball, to keep silent and perfectly still. Any yelp or whimper only fed the hurricane.

It was Mum who really suffered in the end. He remembered, later that Christmas night, the red flashes of the ambulance as they pierced the curtains, bouncing off the internal walls. He had looked out, one arm still shielding Sean, and saw his mother strapped to a bed, her face beyond recognition. And Tom saw from her eyes, even through her bloody mask, that some vital force had already departed — that she would never be the same.

'Where's Mummy going?' asked Sean.

'Away,' said Tom, his little mind gripping onto one truth for dear life: the powerful could not be trusted and the suffering needed a friend.

6

Mossy Mountain

The next morning Tom woke to the sound of rain hitting the tin roof with great force — not cats and dogs, he decided, but larger, more boisterous creatures. After breakfast, there had been lively discussions between the priests about whether it was possible to strike out for Mossy Mountain on such a day. No sooner had the conversation moved to the fieldtrip's inevitable cancellation, than a bright sun broke through the thick cloud, reversing their imminent decision. Still, the air was syrupy with the moisture of the forest, and the ground underfoot was heavy and treacherous.

Again they took a jeepney beyond those roads that formed official maps. This time their vehicle was larger, but to accommodate the entire IFFM and its entourage of drivers, cooks and security guards, half a dozen had to ride on the roof. Both Paul and Tom volunteered for this task, some part of Tom having waited for this since childhood. There was no doubting it: the Philippines seemed to be reintroducing Thomas the Adult to Thomas the Child. Minutes into the ride, a cheek-splitting grin spread across his face, the humid wind whispering through his hair as the vehicle plunged in and out of ditches and culverts. Paul belted him on the upper arm, as if to say, 'Hey, what about this!' Here they now were, in a land beyond seatbelts, clinging white-knuckled onto the roof of a small truck. Time and time again, the jeepney plunged into waterholes, its rear axle spinning deeper into the clay. Every time they thought they were bogged, Tom, Paul and the other men on the roof began to rock the truck to and fro, and somehow this new-found traction made the difference. Tom felt like he was sailing, the vehicle dipping and rising like the bow of a boat in a heavy swell, shrugging off the enormous weight of mud and water that had come across its gunnels in its last dip for the Earth's centre.

The inevitable moment came when the truck would not emerge from the pit. They clambered from the vehicle, initially trying to keep their shoes and clothes clean, but they eventually gave up. Tom waded thigh-high out of the mire towards elevated ground, managing to keep his leather satchel above water level. The driver of the truck seemed unperturbed by the fate of his vehicle, deciding to prop himself under a tree and drink coffee. The rest of the passengers, led by Father Ricardo, moved on towards their destination on foot.

They sludged across the tableland. There was no adequate drainage and it took them well over an hour to progress just a couple of kilometres. Mossy Mountain was the apex of five significant rivers, sourcing Mindanao's rice bowl. Tom began to truly understand this fact: the sheer magnitude, the quantity of water that both entered and traversed the land was beyond calculation. Just that morning's short but heavy downpour made travel almost impossible. *How will these primitive tailings dams stand fast in this watery world?* he wondered. The slash-and-burn practices of the forestry companies had undoubtedly exacerbated the problem. The ancient roots of trees had provided the earth with some form of structure to hold onto, to wedge against, but now the earth was in a state of flux.

At last, the ground began to rise steeply. Rivulets and gullies flowed down and across their path but the footing was better, despite large clumps of clay adhering to the soles of their shoes with each footstep. Tom felt invigorated and surged ahead for the next five hundred metres, nonchalantly passing others. Soon he was level with Father Ricardo.

'A fine day for a walk, Father.'

At first, the priest looked a little surprised to see him there.

'Yes, Thomas,' he said. 'But I should warn you. We still have some eight kilometres to walk and the mountain only gets steeper from here.'

Tom hoped he hadn't gone too hard at the beginning, so he slowed a little. The priest matched his pace and the rest of the group matched the priest's.

'You know, Thomas,' the priest said, 'the people on Mossy Mountain have a hard life. Climbing up and down this mountain is just one example. Their lives are brutal, full of back-breaking work, sickness — the sickness of poverty. In the last twelve months that I have visited the community here, I have personally read the last rites to fifteen people. Thirteen were children, mostly infants. That's a big number, considering there are under fifty people in the whole village.'

They walked in silence while Tom digested what the priest had said. His legs were becoming heavier and his breathing a little harder. The sharp gradient of the climb began to invade his calf muscles. The tendons that joined his lower legs to his ankles seemed to be losing their flexibility, setting like steel with every step. He tried walking on his toes for a while, but this only provided temporary relief. His leather satchel began to dig into his shoulder blades and he cursed himself for bringing it. He could have carried his clipboard and his simple packed lunch separately without this unnecessary weight, he thought, resenting this symbol of his life as a Western academic.

'Thomas, you must know, there is very little that is dignified about these people's existence. We are not Maoists here. We do not idolise the peasantry. There are no noble savages. Some of the environmentalist writings I have read concern me deeply. They place these impoverished communities on a fool's pedestal, as if the villagers know the meaning of life, the way to live. These are marginalised communities which have long lost contact with their heartland … their sense of place.'

'But isn't that exactly what the Company is arguing: to save them from their lot?' Thomas said.

'Yes, the Company and the NPO begin from the same angle, but then we depart from this. As I've told you, the solution is not to stop progress, but to promote *genuine progress* — a progress controlled by the people, not by a transnational company. Not by becoming more ecological, more scientific in a Western sense. This whole environmentalist rubbish is just another form of imperialism.'

Although Tom wanted to convince the priest about his ecological concerns, he didn't want another rehash of this argument. He guessed their small convoy was now a thousand metres or so above sea level. The tops of the remaining stands of forest on the tableland below reminded him of snorkelling over a reef, coral canopies packed tightly together, like giant broccoli. But unlike the smooth watery movement over coral, his body now laboured against the gravity of the mountain. He forced out another line of questioning while hoping that his second wind would come. But his increasing exhaustion made subtle argument more difficult.

'Would you see your position as liberation theology?' Thomas said.

'You ask heavy questions for a man who is labouring up a mountain,' Ricardo laughed. 'Ambiguities are everywhere. There are many positions within Christianity, as there are many in socialism. Maria informed me that she showed you the Green Army. You were interested in our forms of mass mobilisation?' he continued.

'Yes, I saw them,' Tom replied, not sure of what he should tell the priest, or exactly what Maria had reported.

'Well, I don't partake in that form of mass mobilisation.'

'The armed resistance, you mean?'

'Exactly. I involve myself in another form of mass mobilisation.

I try to help the communities to rebuild themselves after their dispossession. I try to provide hope again, to recreate a community. Without community, there is no mass mobilisation. I have seen your protests in Australia. These protests are not community protests; they are the protests of individuals. No sooner do your people gather than they dissipate, returning to their closed fortresses. That is not a society, not a community. That is simply a marketplace. Change in the Philippines is only possible if the communities become strong again, if they are fed, sheltered and re-educated about their needs and wants.'

'You call it re-education,' Tom said. 'If the Company did this, we'd label it propaganda.'

The priest seemed a little taken aback at this last comment. He shrugged.

'I hope you can see the difference. HMC wants the B'laan's land, their resources. My organisation wants the people to have their own resources. It is not a word game. There are differences in these positions that even a blind man can see. Anyway, call it what you like. I have told you before, this is an ideological war. And the people are caught in a vice.'

Tom's legs were beginning to turn to jelly and he was sweating profusely. He wanted to finish the conversation. He could no longer keep up with Ricardo's pace, either physically or cerebrally. He wanted to come up with something that could provide a full-stop to the conversation, preferably something astute, witty or, at least, polite.

Instead he lobbed another big question. 'Could it be that by being part of two communities — the Church and a revolutionary people's organisation — you avoid being so easily pigeonholed, so easily judged by each organisation?'

'Ah, Thomas. Already, you know me too well!' He smiled to show that Tom hadn't pushed too far. Then the priest turned to face the top of the mountain and forged up the path as if he had found some new form of overdrive.

At this point, Tom began to weaken dramatically. His body ached and he could hardly lift his legs. The pride he had exhibited earlier in passing all and sundry in his eagerness to lead from the front quickly gave way to embarrassment. He felt big and awkward, his rangy frame hopelessly out of its element. The lithe bodies of the Mindanao people passed him, seemingly with no effort. But they offered no assistance. Not even Paul stopped.

'You alright, Tom?' Paul breathlessly grunted as he passed. But he continued without waiting for an answer.

Tom imagined a smirk here and a derisory comment there, though he had no evidence for his suspicions. Lights began to twinkle before his eyes. He felt faint, like he was about to vomit, and sunk to his knees, gasping for breath.

He didn't know whether he'd blacked out or not, but if he had it had only been for a few seconds. The rear of the column of hikers was still in his immediate view. He remembered an all-encompassing sickness that had once overwhelmed him at sea in a small sailboat outside the Heads of the Bay back home. He'd very nearly slid from the boat into the water, kilometres from shore, just to seek an end to its torment. This was how he felt now.

It was Maria who tended to him. She opened two sachets of salt and emptied these into his canteen. When he properly regained his senses, he knew that he had been muttering 'I'm sorry, I'm so very sorry' over and over again. He was not quite sure of what he was apologising about. Maria told him to be quiet, to drink and rest. She wiped the sweat from his head with a handkerchief dipped in spit.

'Drink the rest of this. Rest a little. Don't worry, your body is not used to the altitude. And when you are ready, start to climb again,' she told him. 'Here, take off your shoes.'

But he couldn't. Realising this, she pulled them from his feet, banged them against a rock to rid them of their burden of clay, and then tied them together to his satchel.

'You will be much better without them,' Maria said. 'They are too heavy. I must follow the others now. They will need me at the summit. See you soon, okay?'

He nodded and smiled as best he could. Maria walked a couple of paces, looked up at the mountain above her and then returned to the forlorn figure, as if she had forgotten something. As he looked up at her she bent down over him, small beads of perspiration beginning to gather on her neck, and kissed him on the crown of the head.

And then she was gone.

As she disappeared beyond his line of sight an enormous happiness welled up within him. He fought the initial desire to chase after her, telling himself to rest for ten minutes or so while her elixir did its job. He fell back to the earth and looked up at the sky.

Rain clouds moved briskly across the sun.

* * *

The track reached a ridge at last and it meandered before him. Much of the pain in his lungs had subsided now that he was no longer walking up such a steep incline. The electrolytes must have kicked in and this, coupled with the knowledge that he was going to finish the walk, made his heart skip. Once again, he was reminded that even in desperate circumstances joy always managed to bubble through the cracks of his soul. It may have to drift through a quagmire of pain and suffering but, ultimately, his love of life took the upper hand.

He tramped along at a good pace now. There was still no sign of anyone ahead. From on top of the cleared range he looked down into the remnant copses of forest below and spotted an eagle circling. He wondered if it was the same one he'd seen in the days before. The delicate tips of its feathers moved minutely in response to invisible currents. He moved down a slight decline and nearly slipped again, despite the improved traction of his bare feet. Then the path climbed again, not as sharply as before, but enough to feel the stretching of his taut calf muscles. His feet were bruised and sore, and although he began to pant once more, the feelings of weakness had diminished.

Back on top of the ridge again, he caught a glimpse of another grove of huge trees, their buttresses big enough to hold up the walls of cathedrals. This was the last patch of forest before the sky. He was running out of track, of places to go. He wondered if he'd missed the path. Was there a turn-off he hadn't seen? But he consoled himself with an act of basic reasoning: others had freshly chopped up the earth where he stood. In less than five minutes he saw the outline of a village tucked into a clearing of no more than half a hectare. It sat between the last vestige of forest to its north and east, and the crag of the mountain to the west.

The final section of the path was more of a land bridge. Coming from the south, there was a sheer drop on one side — at least five thousand feet — and stunted forest on the other, somehow clinging to the final twenty metres of vertical cliff face before the summit. No doubt the B'laan intended it as the last line of defence, a rare place where their enemies were more vulnerable than they were. He hoped Father Ricardo's troupe, or the Green Army — perhaps both — had already made contact with the tribe. Sudden fear prickled his neck and ears. Every muscle tensed, ready for a poisoned dart or an arrow. He spoke to his anonymous friend: 'Please let me be delivered home to my family again. Don't take me now.'

Standing about fifty metres from the first hut in the village, he saw that the buildings were crisscrossed with woven reeds attached to rough-hewn timber frames. As he got closer he counted eighteen such huts, some much larger than the others. Just before the village proper was a field under cultivation. It took up about half the available area, full of shoulder-high vegetation. He recognised corn and bananas, and some sort of yam or sweet potato. Feeding this field was a small stream, impossibly clear. It appeared to be the villagers' only water source.

Stepping nervously around the corner of the hut closest to the path, he felt his fear partly dissolve. He saw the other members of his group, minus Father Ricardo, sitting under the shade of a large open-air hut, an axis point around which all of the other buildings were facing.

'Hi!' Tom called out, elated. 'Finally made it!'

But instead of heartfelt welcomes he was greeted by a universal 'Shhhhhh!' He immediately went back on alert and, with shoulders hunched and hands quizzically outstretched, he approached them. Maria was first to speak.

'Sit down, Thomas. We are waiting.'

He was so pleased to be able to rest that he no longer cared about the mystery of the situation. He threw down his leather satchel, silently admonishing it as if it were a person. He reached for his water bottle, lay down on his back, rested his head on the bag and relished his immobility beneath the woven roof of the shelter.

'Where's Father Ricardo?' he asked Paul, who was sitting next to him.

'Well, it was really curious when we first arrived here. Absolute silence. But the fire pit over there was still steaming under moist dirt that had just been thrown on it. Father has gone to see what's up. He thinks that the colonel might not have been able to get through to tell them of our arrival.'

'Shit,' Tom said.

Paul passed him a handful of rice. 'Sorry I couldn't stop for you, mate. Had my own shit going on.'

'No worries.' Tom nibbled at the rice not out of hunger but from a primal survival instinct. He took another slug from his water bottle and then shut his eyes. He lost consciousness very quickly.

He awoke on his side, his chin damp with dribble. He was busting to urinate. Most of the others were resting, except Maria, who was smoking as usual. He crawled over to her. 'Maria, which hut is the toilet?'

'Toilet?' she spat. 'Can't you hold on?'

'Uh ... no.'

'Very well. The toilet is there.' She waved her hand expansively.

'Where?'

'There. Everywhere. Just find a spot in the plantain field. But please try to stay out of sight. And be quiet!'

He walked gingerly back towards the field and the entrance to the village. He moved carefully between the banana plants, wincing at every rustling noise he made. No sooner did he unzip his fly than the contents of his disturbed insides rushed out, spraying the heels of his feet. With nose upturned, he covered the excrement with soil that had been piled high in rows around the base of each plant. He peeled a leaf off a plant and wiped his heels, then his backside.

He was on his way to the small stream to wash his hands when a loud cry rent the sky, sending shivers up his spine. He was still looking for the source of the noise when people with muddied faces and bows and arrows began rushing out of the forest on the precipice. They surged towards the clearing where the others in the IFFM party were, and surrounded the meeting ground at the base of the communal canopy.

Tom ducked for cover in the plantain field and jumped low into the place he had just covered up. The smell hit his nostrils with full force. He moved a large banana frond from his view and saw, with some relief, Father Ricardo in urgent conversation with some of the B'laan warriors.

In the middle of his vigil, he felt a tap on his back, and when he looked up he saw a man covered in black and ochre paint staring down at him. The B'laan motioned that he get up off the ground. As soon as he stood, terrified and shaking, the warrior grabbed him by the arm — not forcefully, but providing direction — and led him out of the field towards the others.

Of course, the villagers knew Father Ricardo but they remained disturbed by the foreigner's presence. Briefly, the priest explained to them the purpose of their visit. Soon, a broad smile returned to Ricardo's face.

'Dr McMahon, come over here,' he yelled. 'The chief and his son want to meet you.'

As Tom approached the central group the priest said to him, as an aside, 'You were lucky. They thought you were the Company ... lucky not to take an arrow in your side.'

The priest was rejoicing in making him squirm a little, feeding on his nervousness, his fear.

'Dr Thomas McMahon,' Father Ricardo said, 'this is Chief Tifu Abulu. And this is his son, Timon.'

Tom looked around the gathering. The men were dressed for battle. They had smudged earth across their faces and bodies. The lines of their shoulders and hips were broken with pieces of foliage, creating a camouflage. In the centre of their foreheads was a splash of deep red, highlighting the whiteness and iridescence of their eyes.

After all the introductions, some of the B'laan led them to an enclosed hut, offered them water and food — boiled and mashed sweet potato — then led them back to the village centre. They sat where the priest directed them, and so began a lengthy exchange. Whenever the chief spoke, he spoke in song. The sounds erupting from the chief's mouth were guttural, vital — almost frightening to Tom. The order, the structure of sound was so utterly different here. No eight-note octaves, no arpeggios. Instead, a series of clicks and notes.

It was Timon who interpreted the song for Ricardo and Paul, re-arranging the sounds into words and forming sentences. The chief's son was a tall, willowy man, probably in his mid-twenties. Despite his relative youth, his arched brow, intelligent eyes and definitive movements gave him the bearing of a natural leader.

It seemed that Paul had grasped the basics of the indigenous dialect. *He's full of surprises*, Tom thought. The task of translating the song into a form of B'laan language so that they could understand seemed arduous. On many occasions, the son re-engaged his father, seeking guidance as to the meaning, the correct way of interpreting the phrases of the song. In the end, this process took over half an hour. Members of the IFFM team began to move about on the floor, seeking a position which could provide them with less discomfort, while the painted men sat silently, not moving, not blinking.

At last, the priest turned to the group. Instead of speaking English, he spoke in Filipino to Maria and the other nationals in the group. This only took five minutes, with Maria nodding vigorously the entire time.

At last it was time to translate into English. Father Ricardo was the key. He seemed to be a one-man tower of Babel, the keystone in the arch that spanned across cultures, across millennia.

'Thomas, you are last,' said the priest.

Tom raised his hand to ask a question, but before he could utter a word Ricardo waved him down.

'We have no time for interruptions. Just time enough for me to explain what is happening,' Father Ricardo said. 'You must listen. And then we will respond. The chief, as you probably know, communicates in song on important occasions. His son, Timon, has translated it for us. This is not just an act of simple interpretation. For this is the song of his people: their past, their current position and his aspirations for their future. Much of the song is overlaid with symbols and metaphors with spiritual meaning … creation stories that need to be decoded and unravelled. He was only willing to tell me this story as he understands that I am a holy man, so we are very privileged to be told, to be sung this songline.'

'The important part of the song for us is the protagonist, a young man called Tifu — like the chief,' continued Father Ricardo. 'All was well with the B'laan people. They lived a life in paradise. There was beauty and plenitude everywhere. One day, while Tifu was out hunting deep in the forest, a man called God appeared. God was strangely dressed and his skin was as pale as a dove's. God gave Tifu the Christian Bible and instructed him to take it back to his village straight away and give it to his chief, telling him that the book had the truth of life between its covers. Tifu told God he would. But Tifu had never seen a book before and was not convinced that all truth could be found within such an inanimate object when all around him sang the forest, the sky, the earth and the wind. Still, he decided to do as God had told him. But first he was hungry, so lingered in the forest long enough to shoot a wild boar with his bow and arrow. He was so ravenous that he ate the entire boar uncooked, bones and all, and then fell fast asleep. When he awoke he gathered his hunting equipment, but forgot about the book that was left sitting on a fallen tree trunk. Halfway back to the village he remembered it, but when he returned the book had vanished.'

The priest looked at Tom and Paul. 'The chief believes that this story explains why God has forsaken the B'laan. This explains their forced migration from the lowlands into the highlands over the past hundred years, and why these new oppressors face them — the military and the Company. It is a punishment from God.'

'So they're blaming themselves for their position?' asked Paul.

'Unfortunately, yes. But there is more. The B'laan believe that this is their final stand. That this is their final verse. And that they have nothing left to lose other than their lives. The men surrounding you are Bagani warriors. The military, under instruction from the Company, has placed an order for them to be shot on sight. That is why they were understandably uneasy when they saw the Westerner in our group. The warriors have all taken a sacred oath from their creation song, which has never been invoked before. It is the final oath, the oath of death. You can see the mark of death between their eyes: the ochre. It is called *Dyandi*. They have taken an oath to fight to the last drop of blood. The Company may win, but they must kill the B'laan first.'

The enormous gravity of the situation struck Tom. In Australia, they fought the Company on roundtables. They spoke of best-practice management, carbon trading and ecological diversity. Sometimes the people marched together in the streets, protesting the hazards of nuclear waste or to protect a threatened stand of wilderness. But they were always safe; they always returned home. Here, in a tiny village on the edge of existence, a place beyond markets, the people fought with their lives, expecting to die.

Dyandi. To the last drop of blood.

Finally, there was silence. Eyes refocused on the chief. The same chain of command began again: the chief, his son, the priest in Filipino, then the priest in English.

'Thomas, the chief asks if you have anything to share. Sharing is very important to the B'laan.'

'I have a small bag of boiled rice,' Tom replied tentatively.

'No — not food,' Paul said. 'Perhaps you have a song or a story. The chief wishes to hear the story of the place where you come from.'

Tom ran through the limited hit parade residing in his head. The problem was that the concept of place for him and his people was such an ambiguous thing. Australians were true children of the global diaspora. Tom thought that most of them didn't know where their grandparents were buried. For that matter, although he had visited his mother's grave once as a child, his father was probably dead too by now, and Tom was none the wiser as to where his earthly remains lay hidden.

But he knew that this was not the time for such deliberation. As Ricardo had said, it was about sharing. He had a couple of Irish ballads from his mother's side, but then he worried that these were not sufficiently Australian; they didn't come close to displaying the full ethnic fabric of the nation. He could only come up with 'Waltzing Matilda', the popular song written by Banjo Paterson. It was the unofficial national hymn for Australia, the song that most Australians of his generation knew the words of, while they fumbled around the edges of the official anthem.

He looked at Paul for approval as he began the first lines. Paul grinned and shrugged his shoulders, noncommittal. Tom always thought that what he lacked in tune and tone he made up for with noise. By the third verse, his confidence growing, he was really belting it out. By the time he'd finished, he could hear young children crying in nearby huts, while the warriors' jaws had dropped in astonishment.

He sat down, assuming that his role in the sharing ceremony was over. The silence continued, however, and open mouths continued to gape in his direction. The priest spoke to the chief's son, the son to the chief, the chief back to the son, the son back to the priest. Then, finally, the priest said to Tom, 'The chief wants to know what it means.'

Tom scratched his head and looked to Paul again, who responded with the same shrug as earlier. He didn't really know what it meant, despite the fact that he'd been singing it for years. He didn't really know if any Australians sang the song with a sense of its meaning. But this was no place for subtleties.

'It's about a swagman,' he began.

The priest asked, 'What's that?'

He thought for a moment, seeking the right words to fit into the current context.

'A type of itinerant peasant,' he said.

'Nice work!' Paul declared, tongue-in-cheek.

They followed the now usual pathways of communication, and he sighed with relief when the chief nodded to his son's explanation. Tom was struck by the pure connection that linked father and son. He swallowed hard at the memory of his own loss.

At the same time, Tom laughed inside when he thought of the scrambled state of the song by the time the chief had digested it. Somehow, the humour of the situation made him relax.

He quickly gave up the goal of accuracy in interpretation. Instead, he tried putting it into the Marxist language of the NPA that he'd heard so often since coming to the Philippines.

'It's about this itinerant peasant called Swagman. He's very hungry but there is little to eat, as the ruling class owns most of the land and nearly all of the food. He decides to camp ... rest ... by a billabong — a waterhole — under the shade of a Coolabah tree. Then, luckily for him, along comes a jumbuck — a sheep — and he kills it and eats it. Unfortunately, the landowner — one of the elite — finds out and has the peasant, Swagman, killed by the military. In the end, the ghost — the spirit — of Swagman lives by the waterhole, singing his song: "You'll come a-waltzing Matilda with me." So, I suppose the spirit lives on ... we are not alone. The struggle is everywhere,' he added, hoping to cast some form of meaning over the story.

Again, explanations and interpretations went to and fro. At last there was silence. All watched the chief, Tifu. He murmured something to his son. It came back to Tom.

'Tifu wants to know ... what is a sheep?'

'A type of goat,' interjected Paul.

The definition went back to the chief. After a final period of deliberation he arose, all the time talking animatedly to his son. He came directly towards Tom. The son motioned him to stand. Tifu took his hands and shook them with vigour, and then embraced him. His son spoke seriously to Ricardo one final time and then the priest, smiling with relief more than anything else, said, 'The chief wants you to know that the B'laan also have such a story ... but they have a goat instead of a sheep.'

But the sharing of the songlines and the warm exchanges did not continue for long. The rain clouds gathered for their own mountaintop meeting. Thick mist began to envelop the eyrie that was the home of the B'laan people of Mossy Mountain, and then droplets the size of marbles began to fall. Suddenly, the Mission was mustered for departure.

'If we don't leave now, we'll never get down the mountain. Now that the trees are gone there'll be flash-flooding,' Maria explained.

They threw their bags over their shoulders and said their hasty goodbyes. Before they plunged down the ridge track, the son of the chief ran to shake Tom's hand. He then grabbed him quite fiercely by the wrists, motioning to Ricardo for one last act of translation.

'The chief's son wants to know why God made you so powerful and the B'laan so powerless?'

'Which god?' responded Tom, thinking on his feet.

'God. The one God. The Almighty,' interpreted Ricardo.

'Tell him I don't believe in such a god,' Tom said. 'Tell him I believe in the B'laan. I believe in the living.'

Ricardo looked at him slightly askance and remained silent.

* * *

Within twenty minutes, the drops had turned to waterfalls. Covered from head to foot in mud, the members of the Mission began to scoot on their backsides down the mountain.

Tom felt strangely elated, centred. There was no sign of the earlier exhaustion that had crippled him. They reached a river that had been only a stream that morning. As they stood on the bank, weighing up the best place to enter the watery fray, a four-wheel drive with the HMC logo pulled up. The PR officer for HMC, Jenny Thompson, sat in the passenger seat.

'A lift, Dr McMahon? A lift, Father?' she said.

Tom moved towards the car without thinking. A vice-like grip took hold of his arm. It was the priest.

'No thank you, Ms Thompson. The people don't need you. We don't want your assistance.'

With this sharp dismissal, she wound up her window and issued an order to the driver. The car ploughed through the rushing water now full of mud, branches and dangerous debris.

'But,' said the priest to Tom, out of the side of his mouth, 'we enjoyed eating your rice and shitting in your toilets.'

7

Birth and Death

In the middle of preparations for their departure from Bampakan back to General Santos City, a B'laan delegation arrived at the parish compound. The delegation was led by the chief's son, Timon. He looked first at the priest, his eyes earnest and pleading. Paul, sitting next to Tom, provided him with the rudiments of the translation. Timon had come to beg the IFFM to return to Mossy Mountain, as intelligence from the Green Army told them that a raid on their village was imminent. It was believed that the military would not attack if the members of the Mission were there.

Father Ricardo spoke to Timon and then repeated his words in English. 'I told him I was sorry, but that the Mission is near its end. We are due in Manila the day after next. I cannot break with these commitments.'

Timon lunged towards Tom's side, tugging at his sleeve and speaking rapidly with great purpose. Tom looked to Paul for help.

'He says, "Please, Dr McMahon. If you come they will not attack us ... they will not attack when you are there."'

All parties looked back to Father Ricardo. But the priest shook his head, ending the conversation, and left the room.

That night, sharing the room with the tribal warriors, Tom slept uncomfortably. Throughout the night the warriors spoke agitatedly to one another and smoked clove-smelling cigars, the whole time stealing glances at him and the curate as they twisted and turned on their beds.

Around dawn, Tom woke sharply in a sweat. Looking across the floor of his room, he could see the tribal warriors curled up together, sleeping. Any look of fierceness had gone. Their vulnerability touched him deeply. Without warning, tears welled up in his eyes, his throat constricting. For the first time, he seriously asked himself whether he could afford to stay on. He decided that he must find a phone to discuss the situation with Amanda.

From the beginning it went badly. Following the wooden greetings, Tom got to the point:

'Amanda, I just thought I'd, er, let you know that there may be a change of—'

'What now, Tom?'

'I haven't made up my mind yet,' he continued, skirting around the inevitable. 'It's just that things are rather desperate here. It's a long story, but the people of one of the villages fear for their immediate safety. Their leaders believe our presence will ease the danger ... that nothing will happen while we're there.'

Tom felt the silence almost choke the phone line.

Finally Amanda spoke, her voice cold. 'What about your work, Tom? And my work? The university. I'm off to London at the end of next week ... What about *us*?' she added, quietly.

Again there was a hush. Then she continued. 'So what you're saying is, distinct from *discussing* the situation with me, you're *telling* me that you're not coming home.'

'Look ... don't be like that.' She's right, this isn't a request at all, he thought guiltily.

'Like what? It's not all beer and skittles here you know. The kids have been sick—'

'What sort of sick?' he interjected, suddenly panicked.

'Just colds.' She changed tack. 'Look, I think you've done your time there. Come home now or don't bother coming home at all.'

And with that, the line cut out. He dialled the number again, only to hear Jem's recorded voice telling anyone who would listen that no-one was home. Tom stood frozen, considering whether to try again. He decided against it.

Back in his room, he laboured over the conversation with Amanda, stomach churning. He knew his marriage stood on a precipice. Perhaps, unconsciously, he had pressed Amanda to this point, positioned them both in a place where she had to make an ultimatum. Or even worse, he thought, he'd pushed her to be the initiator once again, while he played the same old passive part in their relationship. After an hour of hand-wringing, and rewinding and replaying sound bites of their conversation, Tom grew tired of himself.

He switched into work mode and rifled through his obligations in his diary. He decided another week may be the difference between life and death for the B'laan of Mossy Mountain, and there was nothing in his life — not even his family — that couldn't wait a week.

The clincher came at breakfast. He made his approach to the priest, who replied, 'Thomas, you are truly *sharing* the burden of the people. As you know, I cannot stay in Mindanao at the present. I would be concerned to leave you here without my protection. Enrico and the NPO have placed you under my care.'

'But Father, Paul and I can accompany Dr McMahon,' Maria said. 'I know the area well and Paul understands the language well enough.' She seemed delighted to learn of Tom's interest in the new plan.

'There will be no further demands placed upon you or the Church — you have done your job well,' Maria said to the priest. 'I will speak to Colonel Sichon and place Dr McMahon directly under his command.'

She then suggested that her journalistic talents would be most useful in such a situation, as further mileage could be made of Dr McMahon's continued presence in Mindanao in the national press. 'I will report this situation back at NPO headquarters when I return to Manila.'

When Tom told Paul the new plan, Paul said, 'Are you sure the delicious Maria Cortes has nothing to do with it?'

With anyone else, Tom wouldn't have tolerated this invasion of his personal life. He responded with care. 'Look, I won't deny that Maria's presence is a pleasant one. But it only adds to the decision that I'd already made this morning.'

'It's just that you're a long way from home, and anything can happen. Tom, you've got to stand back and take a cold hard look at the situation. Don't jeopardise what you've got for something that may be forgotten in a week's time.'

'I do appreciate your concern,' Tom said. 'I rang Amanda this morning to try and explain. To sort things out. But I think we're past that point now. And Maria or no Maria, I'm going.'

He didn't persist with denials. He felt elated that Maria was coming along and he knew in his own heart, or believed he did, that Maria's presence was a wonderful extra. It was not, however, the reason he was staying.

* * *

The trip back up Mossy Mountain began in earnest that afternoon. By evening the small party had once more reached the village high in the mountains. Tom travelled lightly this time, at a measured pace, impressing himself with his adjustment to altitude in just a few days.

The villagers welcomed their guests. On the first night, there was abundant food, mostly variations of plantain, and much tribal music driven by constant drumming. Following the welcoming festivities, Tom noticed that he and Paul were being ushered to a hut shared by the village's single men. In the middle of the hut a fire pit, designed for warmth in this higher climate, also kept mosquitoes at bay. Tom felt very grateful for his bed.

For the first couple of days, Tom felt a little uneasy as he tried to fit in to village life. He decided that he might be of help lugging the water from the well to the huts. And then, after he'd made the exhausting trip up the hill a dozen times or more, he switched to collecting dead wood from the forest floor, stacking it on a ready-made pile situated at the heart of the village.

After a morning of backbreaking work, Maria came up to him and told him to stop, as this was the women's work. He said to her, sweat pouring from him, 'Why didn't you tell me earlier?'

She replied with a twisted smile, 'Oh ... you looked like you were enjoying yourself.'

But it wasn't enjoyment he felt; it was anxiety that fluttered around in his stomach. Some of this tension, he decided, he inherited from the villagers themselves. They seemed on edge, as if an attack could take place at any time. People darted fearful glances at any sound out of the familiar. The Bagani warriors wore battle dress the whole time, their faces twisted with painted anger. Sentries were placed high in the trees above the land bridge, the only place of entry.

This anxiety fed Tom's other concerns, and he worried at times about his family, his job, how he would sort things out when he returned. He thought about Amanda and the years they had spent together, and contemplated his future alone. *What will I do without my old guiding light?* he asked himself. Periodically his mind would lurch to the saddest, most difficult place of all: the prospect of his children living through a separation.

After a few days the villagers seemed to relax a little, feeling that the threat may have subsided. Tom now picked up the basic customs of the village relatively easily. Most of them made sense without the need for an overly complex set of rules, as was the case, he decided, in his society. The village went to bed just after nightfall and awoke with the sun. There were no alarms or sirens, no planes or trains. The silence of nightfall was bottomless. He found he had never slept better in his life.

In the mornings they took their time over a simple breakfast. For milk and butter, and for ploughing the fields, the villagers kept water buffalos. They made pancakes by combining dairy products with wild maize and these, along with sweet potatoes, formed the main diet. Occasionally, a rough and chewy rice also made its way up the mountain, a result of trade in the lowlands. Tom loved the fruits and vegetables from the communal garden that complemented these staples. Sometimes meat was included when the men were lucky enough to come back after a hunting trip with a pig, a bird or other small game.

For the bulk of the day, the men and women pursued separate tasks. Maria worked with the women as they tended the field, constantly weeding, harvesting and carrying water to it. Half of the men still stood vigil against the possibility of attack, hidden in the forest. Those men not on watch usually hunted in the mornings, napped in the middle of the day and met in the communal hut in the afternoons.

Tom was invited to these meetings but rarely understood the nature of proceedings. Paul explained to him that it was at these meetings where most of the decision-making of the village took place. The structure of the meetings was always the same. The chief sat in the place of prominence — closest to the fire — with his son Timon to his side. Sometimes the chief sang like he had on Tom's first trip here, his voice rising with the smoke. At other times, it was Timon who did most of the talking. Whenever Tom saw the chief's son these days, he was wearing what Paul had described as 'his full paint-and-battle-dress': a stunning magenta plume of feathers attached to his head, no doubt denoting his princely status.

Sometimes Paul mumbled bits and pieces by way of interpretation, but after a while Tom didn't look to him for help any more. Tom decided that life without language suited him for now. So much of it now appeared unnecessary. Sometimes during these men's meetings he would go off into a trance, staring at a palm frond or at a bird sipping pollen in the top storeys of the forest.

Everything seemed so clear, the edges so well-defined. Beauty here seemed more intense, danger more accessible, more acceptable. Tom felt as if the intensity of his existence had been heightened. He was now living in a world where pleasure and pain were less ambiguous, but more intertwined.

Within these borders of danger, Tom felt oddly at peace. Without language there was still a deep poetry of communication taking place, through a sequence of universal signs and noises, and plenty of smiles. He thought back to when he had first seen the documentary in Australia, made by Jack Collins — his boyhood friend — that had kicked off this whole experience, first alerting him to the B'laan's battle against HMC. It was Jack also who helped him initiate contact with the National People's Organisation in Manila.

Bizarrely, Tom remembered, the program had come onto television on the very same evening of the day of the monumental meeting at the Environment Centre, when Patrick Walters had gone ballistic at both Louise and the HMC crew. Tom had just lain down on the living room couch at home — flicking through the channels, seeking balm for his harried mind — when something startling happened. A face shone out at him, a B'laan woman with eyes of deep brown, deep-rooted in pain and despair. Without words, she had spoken directly to him. His chin dropped, his mind buckled, as if the woman's face alone had made a decision for him. For half an hour he sat transfixed. And when he'd gone to bed that night, he'd shut his eyes and felt the faces of the B'laan people burned into his soul.

In the flesh their presence was even more splendid. Beaming smiles chipped at the edges of his stony heart. And when he felt like conversation, there was Paul and Maria.

Since they'd come to the village, Tom never saw Maria without her purple sarong, while Paul usually wore a black Micky Mouse t-shirt and a pair of shorts. No-one wore shoes here.

* * *

They had been in the village for nearly a week, when one morning the three of them went out into the forest to collect firewood. They walked for over a mile across the mountain ridges before they came across any deadwood fit for burning.

'You see how far the people must travel for fuel?' Maria said. 'All the wood closer to camp has already been collected. Each day the people must walk further.'

It seemed that Maria had decided to take on the mantle of the priest. Often Tom felt on the receiving end of a sermon. No doubt Maria had decided he still needed educating.

'What else do they use for fuel?' Tom asked.

'Buffalo shit,' Paul chimed in. 'They wind it up in coils. Dry it out in the sun. Burns for hours.'

They walked on. Tom held both his arms out, while Paul and Maria saddled him up with pieces of wood. It started to get heavy and Tom knew he'd have to carry it the mile or so back to the village. Maria lifted another large piece onto the pile.

'Easy on, Maria,' he said. 'There's more than enough fuel here to contribute to global warming.'

'Fuck global warming!' she said. Tom felt that again his attempt at humour had fallen on deaf ears. Jumping across the forest floor in a frenzy, Maria now decided to load him up with more and more.

'Um, I think he was just joking, Maria,' Paul said. 'Anyway, we've got more than enough now.'

'How is it a joke? Hasn't the penny dropped for you, Thomas? You First World Greenies throw all your efforts into your precious climate change campaigns, promising an Armageddon. But guess what? Armageddon came here a long time ago. It's not about fucking melting icecaps here. Just ask the villagers.'

Obviously, Tom realised, he'd struck a raw nerve. There seemed to be quite a number of them, and he never knew until it was too late that he had hit another one.

When Maria thumped down the last piece hard, Tom dropped the whole load in protest. 'Maria ... I'm trying to learn,' he said.

She gathered some wood from the fallen pile and set off at breakneck speed.

'Maria!' he yelled. But she was gone.

He started after her, but Paul said, 'Don't worry. Let her go. She'll calm down eventually. Always does.'

The two men gathered the remaining fuel and headed back across the range. Sometimes the shadow of the huge peak of Mossy Mountain moved over them and, at other times, they emerged into sunlit clearings. Tom noticed enormous changes in temperature between the two spaces.

'You'll have to forgive Maria,' Paul said after they'd been silent for some time. 'It's incredibly hard being a woman in this gig.'

'I reckon it would be.'

'And that stuff about climate change. I should've told you on the plane. Go easy with that stuff here.'

'What?'

'I remember the environmentalists were big on it in Australia when I was out there.'

'But can't you see it's all connected?' Tom said. 'Too much industrialisation. Too much unfettered growth. Climate just connects these issues — connects the dots.'

'And clouds others. Look Tom, you've got to understand, nothing's *post-industrial* here. Maria and the others in the NPO, I've heard them talking and they just see it as another way for the wealthy world to discipline the poor. And I can't help agreeing with them, to tell you the honest truth. It seems to me that climate takes the *politics* out of it. Makes it nature versus people. But it's people versus people.'

Paul pointed at Tom and said, 'You can see that now, surely. The Company against *us*. Don't lose sight of that. It's about the dispossession of our people, not about a flood that might come one day.'

* * *

Because of his foreigner status, no eyebrows rose whenever Tom left the men's company to help the women in the garden. Sometimes he carried the water for them. He'd decided he didn't care if it was women's work or not. The younger women giggled when he struggled with the large container, for he could not mimic their ease of carrying the water above their heads.

The women worked incredibly hard, all the time tending to the children and the animals, or gathering food from the field or forest. When their work was done they began the task of preparing the main meal for the village, eaten in the evenings, all together, at one sitting.

It was during these times with the women in the garden that Tom learned more about Maria's life, though she did not willingly reveal too much about her past. Her story came out in short bursts.

She was the eldest of nine children. Her father had died in an industrial accident when she was eight. Living in Manila, she had left school at fifteen to help her mother feed her siblings. At sixteen she married a much older man who promised to provide for her mother and family. He too died an untimely death, but left her with enough money to relieve her mother of her burden and for Maria to return to school. She managed to get a cadetship with the General Santos City regional newspaper at eighteen, and so began her working life as a journalist. Her involvement in radical politics was gradual. Now, at thirty-three, she was less active than she had been when in her mid-twenties, but she still held rank in the Green Army.

Whenever he and Maria talked, Tom was conscious that the women were watching them closely and commenting on their relationship. He noticed how the villagers often thrust them together at meals and in the fields.

Tom felt hopeless when he was in Maria's company, clumsy and unsure. Even in the garden, she was frighteningly competent. Her wrists flicked deftly at the weeds or harvested the crop with a minimum of effort and fuss. Although her body was small, she was strong and well-coordinated. Where Tom had to concentrate with every fibre of his being, she could perform tasks while talking or smoking or flicking her hair from her mouth or looking somewhere else.

He liked to crouch in her shadow, feeling her warmth, watching her efficient and definite movements. She never appeared to hesitate, so certain was she of her purpose and the actions needed to achieve it. He sometimes found himself staring at her. Her black hair usually fell about her shoulders. But Tom particularly liked it when she wore it up, highlighting the sensual arc of her neck. And in the absolute clarity of this mountain light — away from the dross of the city — her skin had become quite translucent. She was a striking woman, a woman of immense power.

On the sixth night of their stay, Tom was sleeping in the single men's quarters as usual. His deep sleep was interrupted — a subtle penetration of his dreams at first, then a persistent, repetitive voice which forced him into the land of the living. A dog's incessant screaming demanded immediate action, but no-one in the hut budged. The men not out on patrol snored deeply.

Sliding from his sleeping bag, dressed only in a pair of boxer shorts, he weaved his way between the sleeping bodies. At this time of night, at this altitude, it was surprisingly cold. He retraced his steps to the hut, grabbed the sleeping bag and threw it over his naked torso like a shawl.

Through hooded eyelids, he spotted the dog circling desperately underneath a small bush. She moved as if caught in a cage, but the bars that confined her were invisible. For a while it seemed she was chasing her tail, but her pregnant bulk made that an impossible task. Tom realised how different this dog was to his own pet.

Then it clicked. She was having pups, building an earth nest, hundreds of thousands of years of instinct siphoned into one instant.

He lifted the dog carefully and brought her under a lean-to. She continued to circle wildly, but her yelping had stopped and she seemed comforted by his gentle strokes. He soothed her with sounds that he had used so often to quieten his children. He told her she was safe.

Then there was movement in the corner of his eye. It was Maria, disturbed from her sleep, standing quietly behind his right shoulder, dressed in a long t-shirt. *How long has she been there?* wondered Tom.

She moved forward and knelt down beside him. She kissed him gently on the cheek and then reached for his face. She gently turned his head towards her and looked directly into his eyes, her head moving from side to side, as if she was searching for something within him. She found what she was looking for. Her lips met his.

The dog's bloody waters came. And there was the first of the pups. In an instant, one had become three, easing out of their own accord, each with its own placenta — gory parcels slithering quickly behind.

Immediately, the mother gobbled up these bloody packages in a half-gagging but resolute fashion. Cleaned of mucus and blood, the three pups lay, two black and one a mottled brown. Tom marvelled at their first moments in this universe.

The mother lay on her side again and Tom saw the head of the fourth pup appear. He moved the first three pups to the dog's nipples, and they clung on as she swayed and rocked in the troughs of rhythmic contractions. In an instant, it lay next to its brothers and sister, with the placenta following.

Maria retreated to the cooking hut, threw some fuel on the fire and filled the dog's bowl with water. When she re-entered the labour ward, the sight of five more tiny forms couched in a bloody gel greeted her. Tom smiled broadly.

'Nine pups! And nine placentas! My God, how has she been able to eat in the past weeks?' he said.

His jaw dropped again when he realised the new mother's job was not yet done. Another black pup popped out. The dog looked quite exhausted now. The new lives she had created drew voraciously on her ribcage, sucking even more life from her.

The last pup was the runt. Its entry into life had been in a noose fashioned from the umbilical cord, and Tom wondered if death was near, as this enormous brood contested for the limited life essence of its mother. He placed the runt in the palm of his hand and moved it closer to the mother's teat.

The mother rested now. She lapped feebly from her bowl, as Tom tilted it to one side for easy access. She licked Tom's hand.

When all was done, unease shivered through Tom. He felt that in his own world, in the shine of the stirrups and the language of the medicos, somewhere in the rehearsals of antenatal classes, the magic and the danger of birth — and life itself — had been muted, the edges dulled, the intensity dissipated. Shamefully, he realised that the birth of this nameless dog's litter had filled him with more wonder than that of his own children. Or was this raw and unexpected experience just another excuse to justify his own dreadful shortcomings? All his life he had seized on grand narratives within which he only played bit parts, the script so large it made a mockery of human agency.

Maria gauged his shift of mood, took his hand and held it to her cheek. 'What's wrong, Thomas?'

But he could only shrug his shoulders.

She considered him for a while, deciding the best course of action. She kissed him again. This time her tongue touched his. She took his hand and led him to the field where the vegetables and fruit trees were cultivated. Without hesitation, she took off his shorts and shrugged off her t-shirt. Tom drank in her nakedness: convex and concave in places of magic.

Planting her hands on his chest, she pushed him back onto the damp earth. Without the light of distant cities, the stars hovered and burst above her shoulders.

At that instant he felt part of a larger power, plugged into a universe beyond his understanding. The mountain forest pulsed and its blood pumped through his veins.

At last the violent rutting, bone against bone, ended in a painful dry-retching of his entire being, paroxysms of emptiness. Tom felt her contractions grip him and he tried to smother her mouth with his own, for fear her cries would wake the village.

Their lovemaking complete, she cleaned their bodies with a handful of earth. And then, in between tears, she told him a story.

'Tom, I'm sorry if I get angry with you. But ... it seems to me that you have everything that I haven't. Yet still you aren't happy. You have a wife and children.' She paused for some time as if, Tom felt, she was summoning strength. 'I lost my little darling when she was six. A fever just came onto her ... a Thursday before Easter. On Sunday, instead of eating chocolate eggs with her cousins, she was gone. I held her body in my arms for hours. Until she was cold.'

She told him of a relationship that had ended shortly afterwards and of a pain that still dwelt within her. He rocked her head, her body in his arms, desire gone, only tenderness remaining. They lay in silence into the hours before dawn. Maria's face, so animated most of the time, appeared smooth and serene in stripes of moonlight. Tom had never felt so much at peace, venturing tentatively that perhaps this was happiness. He was always an awkward stranger to its approach.

When sleep began to roll over him, it was not bliss that visited him but a memory. Another piece broke from his soul, scuttling for the surface of his consciousness.

Between the caravan and the cliff there was a cage for his father's hunting dogs. This was the place where Dad sent him for punishment. One dog, the male, didn't like his presence, growling when he entered. The dogs didn't settle until he took his place furthest from the bowl. The roof of the cage was low, which forced him to sit with neck bent, or to move around on all fours. The blistering heat of the day mixed with the smell of the dogs. He was thirsty but each time he moved towards the bowl, the big male growled and raised his hackles. Eventually he would find his place: the bottom of the pack. The other animals sensed it and allowed him his turn at the bowl. He lapped the fetid water full of the pack's saliva.

8

Dyandi

After two weeks, the military had not attacked the village and a sense of safety resumed. Most of the B'laan believed that Tom's presence had been responsible for the peace. In fact, Colonel Sichon and an attachment of his bodyguards from the Green Army had visited them the previous night, reporting that they had witnessed the military withdrawing from the area. To show their appreciation, the tribe planned a feast for that evening.

On the day before Tom's departure, the men made arrangements to go hunting. Timon, again wearing his magnificent pink headdress, found Tom at the little stream having a wash. The villagers had not invited Tom to go hunting before, but Timon presented him with a newly made spear crafted from wood and stone. It became clear he was now to be included in the hunting party.

In bare feet, boxer shorts and a t-shirt, he followed them into the fringes of the forest and then along the mountain's ridge. He may not have looked like a Bagani warrior but he could now, at least, feel like he was *with* them.

The going was slow and the air was humid beneath the canopy. The men moved in single file, with Paul and Tom wedged in between them. Tom chuckled when he thought how appalled some of his cohorts at the Environment Centre would be if they could see him out hunting wild game.

For three hours the march through the thick forest continued, the hunters of the forest floor dodging bark and debris as big as trucks. The men moved in silence, checking animal scats along the way. These piles of droppings provided the hunters with a wealth of information. Whispered conversations followed each fresh discovery, sometimes leading them to change direction or increase their stealth. Tom was included in the huddles. Although he was oblivious to their intricacies, he did manage to learn from Timon's snorting that they were in pursuit of a wild boar. Earlier, he had thought they were chasing small game. The idea that they were after something larger, something dangerous, sent shivers up his spine.

'What do we actually do if the pig charges us?' he asked Paul.

When Paul relayed the question to the others, he caused a good deal of laughter among the men. Paul turned to Tom with a smile on his face. 'They say if the pig charges, then we kill it!'

Timon motioned to them with his hand over his mouth, and the men quickly remembered the importance of silence on the hunt. Still, guffaws snuck out through their fingers covering their mouths. Tom decided to forget about asking any more questions.

About three hours into the hunt, the men cornered the boar in a rocky cleft. Through the language of the forest, they had known of its presence long before Tom saw it. It was Timon who threw the first spear, its bone head wedging in the animal's spine. The pig lashed out, startling Tom as it ran at the circle of men. Each man repelled it with thrusts of his spear, closing the circle even more. With its huge tusks swinging, the pig lunged towards Tom. Dropping his spear, he scampered up the nearest tree. He had never moved so fast. With the circle broken, the pig ran after him, not pausing at the base of the tree, but rampaging through the undergrowth in a desperate bid for freedom.

Three of the hunters flew past the tree after the wild animal. The rest, including Timon, stood in a stunned silence. It was Paul who began laughing first, followed by Timon and then the others. This time, their amusement was so great that two of the lead hunters dropped their weapons and fell to the ground, gripping their bellies with laughter. Just when they began to get some control, Timon pointed at the white man perched in the tree. One of the hunters then re-enacted his inglorious retreat, and the laughter surged again. After a while, even Tom began to laugh nervously. Paul urged him to climb down and when he did Timon, through Paul's translation, assured him that the boar was injured and bleeding, so tracking it would be easy.

* * *

Later that evening, the boar stood on a spit in the middle of a great fire in the centre of the village. Fat from the beast fell and crackled into the flames. Sparks shot high beyond the canopy where they merged, finally, with the glistening stars. The great fire illuminated the villagers. It had been a fretful time for the community, and many of their faces shone with open relief. Hunks of flesh hung from their mouths, though their conversations never diminished. Countless times throughout the evening they recounted the tale, with the Bagani warriors acting out Tom's actions. No matter how many times the story was spun, the hilarity was just the same, with the entire village — men, women and children — united in crescendos of mirth, tears streaming from their eyes. Maria laughed with the loudest, pinching Tom on the cheek, telling him that he was 'a silly boy'.

After most of the eating was done, Timon sat down on the ground next to them, placing his arm around Tom's shoulders. The chief's son called out to Paul, who joined their group for his now-familiar translator's role.

Paul said, 'Timon is saying to you that his father's family and village are deeply indebted to you. That you have been a great spirit, living among them … that you have protected them. You may not be a great hunter, but by your actions you are a great protector. It is this that is truly important.'

Tom found himself responding with some formality, as if moving into ritual mode. 'Tell Timon that it has been my profound pleasure to live among the B'laan. That I have learnt a great deal about life. That he honours me with his words … and that I thank him for his generosity.'

Timon jumped up and walked straight to where his father was sitting, entering into earnest conversation. Maria squeezed Tom's arm and then kissed him on the ear.

'I'm very proud of you, Thomas,' she said. 'You are *my* champion hunter, anyway.'

He felt himself blushing. Since their first kiss, Maria did not seem to care about showing signs of public affection towards him. The women looked at them knowingly, a couple of the younger ones openly tittering.

When Timon had finished the conversation with his father, he looked very serious. He sat down next to Tom again and motioned Paul to join him.

Paul did his best to translate word for word. 'Timon wishes for you to join him, the chief and the other warriors in the men's hut.'

'Of course. But what for?'

'We'll find out soon enough,' said Paul. 'Excuse us, Maria. The mighty hunter has been beckoned!'

* * *

Smoke billowed from a fire located in the men's hut. It was so thick that it took some time before Tom could see much at all. There didn't appear to be any form of ventilation, with the fire flashing every time the blanket overhanging the door was parted, letting in a fresh surge of oxygen.

Once all the men were assembled, the chief began to sing. A high pitch of irregular rhythms blended with the smoke and the oncoming darkness of night. Tom drifted to a place that seemed both extraterrestrial and fiercely of this earth.

Chief Abulu's eyes began to project a mirror image of the fire. At one stage, it appeared to Tom as if flames were shooting from his face directly, as if they weren't a reflection at all. Tom knew he was witnessing a sacred rite: a space where there were times of silence followed by instructed responses.

Finally, the chief moved from his trance. Timon placed an earthenware bowl in front of his father and then handed him a knife. The chief warmed his right hand over the fire and then sliced it deeply across his palm, from his thumb to his smallest finger. Blood lurched into the bowl. The circle of men said something together, a verse of sorts. The chief passed the bowl to his son and Timon repeated the sequence. The vessel passed in the rhythm of the sun, from dawn 'til dusk, each warrior adding his spilt blood to the whole.

It came to rest in front of Paul. He hesitated. Timon spoke to him and Paul whispered something in return. There was a tense verbal exchange, with both of them becoming a little agitated. Eventually, Paul passed the bowl and knife to the warrior sitting on Tom's left without cutting himself. This created quite a stir among the men. Timon demanded that the bowl be handed to Tom. The warrior did so, and gave him the knife. Timon looked to Paul to translate.

'Timon wishes you to understand what is happening here. The warriors are undertaking their oath: the oath of *Dyandi*. They wish that you undertake it.'

Timon and the warriors watched Tom silently.

'I don't want to offend the men. If I can support them by sharing in the ritual then surely that's a good thing.' Tom said.

'Only if you can really live up to the oath,' Paul said. 'To fight for the B'laan until the last drop of blood is left in your body. Can you really do that? I know I can't.'

'I reckon I can fight it in my own way, a way that's different from the B'laan. Back in Australia where the Company's based ... I can hurt them there, I reckon. Anyway, surely it's an honour to be asked?'

'Of course it's an honour. But Tom, would you die for the cause? Would you fight until the last drop of blood?'

'In a manner, yes.'

'I don't think it's symbolic.'

The men began to get restless. Timon spoke to Paul again. But Paul wanted to make his point. It seemed to Tom that Paul's levity had disappeared; his face was pale and solemn.

'Tom, Father Ricardo asked me to look after you. I feel that you and Maria are, in some ways, under my duty of care. There are lots of issues that you haven't had time to consider yet. Perhaps we can ask Timon for some time to think this through. Besides, there are real health concerns associated with partaking in this ritual fully. The men's blood may be infected with many things, strains of—'

Tom had heard enough.

'My own countrymen are directly responsible for these people's suffering — it's the least I can fucking do,' he said. But it was more than that. He felt an urge to move beyond his once closely held reason. He remembered his decision not to take the Eucharist, not to share the bread with the people of Bampakan only a few weeks earlier. It had been a mistake. It had marked him as different, separate from the struggle, detached from the true lives of these individuals, an outsider on some heroic mission to save them.

He increasingly felt that until now he had just been writing a travel novel in his own head — a series of *events* and *encounters*, with

Mindanao cast as the shadow world — roving through time and space, himself some kind of plastic hero with no centre. Ghosts from his past now demanded reckoning, having entered the soft hollowness of his fictional self. But through the politics of his story, passions had been triggered, science blown away. He decided, then and there, that he needed saving too, and that he needed to be one of them.

He imagined himself back at the church in Bampakan and conjured up a different ending to that morning, an ending but also a new beginning. He imagined his body touching those around him in the pungent silence of the mass, local women holding their heads low beneath rainbows of scarves. Suddenly, all those queuing in front of him evaporated and the face of the young curate was grinning at him again. In this version of events, the priest placed the sacrament gently on Tom's tongue, whispering the incantation 'Body of Christ', and as the disc of unleavened bread dissolved, Tom couldn't have cared less about apparent or intended hypocrisy. In fact, he decided that he had never felt so right. He hadn't been reborn. He hadn't seen the true light of God. No, he had simply shared the bread with the people. They were marching together against the darkness.

Solidarity is the power of the powerless, Tom remembered from his conversation with Father Ricardo in General Santos City, when he was still in a sweat after his basketball exploits. This was the people's *only* source of power. By dealing with the Company, or anyone outside its sacred ring, its glue of trust and togetherness would wither. It may have been the only weapon the people had, but it was also the most potent power source of all — a warming liquid ambrosia of communal love, an elixir of oneness, now flowing through his veins, that ache to *belong* for so long. Now, he was part of it and he trusted it. *Amen.*

'Don't worry, Paul,' he said, bringing himself back to the present. 'I'll explain to Father Ricardo that you were very concerned and tried to stop me. But I must accept this honour.'

Paul shrugged, related the decision to Timon and then, looking disconsolate, left the hut. Timon grasped Tom around the shoulders and the other warriors murmured approval.

With the knife, Tom opened his hand painlessly, gladly. Heavy droplets fell into the crimson mass that was already there. Tom watched Timon send the bowl on its circular path once more. At last, it came to rest at the feet of the chief. Again, the chant began. When the silence fell, the chief took the bowl to his lips and drank from it. Tom realised the full extent of what they now expected of him. *This isn't the blood of Christ*, he thought, *this isn't wine — it is the very essence of the B'laan people.* When the bowl came to him, Tom fought the desire to gag as he moved the cup to his lips. When his tongue made contact with the sweet-salty warmth of the mixture his gut lurched in reflex action. Lowering the bowl down in front of him, saliva gushed into his mouth — the precursor to vomit. Fighting hard against the reflex, he did not dare look up at the warriors' faces. Again he summoned his strength of purpose and in a sheer act of will he raised the bowl once more, taking a deep draught of the bloody soup.

Then it was gone. The next man in the line had the bowl in front of him.

9

The Fire

Maria and Tom lay in a puddle of their own making on the forest's periphery, their bodies muddy and bruised. This was their last night together.

He had never felt this way about Amanda, not even at the beginning. In the first flush of romance there is often a time of heightened ardour, but Tom felt this was different. It was more essential with Maria. They traded something elemental between them and sometimes its carnality verged on the brutal. It made Tom feel as if he was desperately gasping for air after being held under water for too long. But the brutality was never cruel. Just when the well appeared empty, one of them reached into its depths and revealed a hidden but renewed supply. In the respite between visits to the well, there was a peace.

'Thomas,' breathed Maria, her energy quite spent, 'are you happy with your life?'

'I don't really think like that.'

Maria rolled away from him, her face towards the clearing. He touched her back, covered with the wet tangle of her hair.

'I'm sorry Maria,' Tom said. 'I'm not being dismissive. It's just that I don't know how I actually feel about these things. Whether I feel happy or sad. Happiness is not something I've ever really looked for.'

She sat up, brushing the dirt from her chest and stomach. 'Do you love your wife, Thomas?'

Tom felt his momentary bliss disappearing. 'You're asking very difficult questions.'

'Jesus Christ — it's a fucking easy question.' She lowered her voice to avoid waking anyone in the village, but retained her vehemence. 'Do you love your wife or not? I have to know. I may not see you again after you leave Manila. I don't just do this with anyone, you know. Who do you think I am? Just some Filipina slut? Someone you can have a little fun with?'

'Of course not. I didn't think that for one minute. I just can't—'

'And you were stupid taking that oath today. Paul told me all about it. Who do you think you are? Just some liberal over in the Third World, playing Mother Teresa. Do you realise what you've just done? You have taken a sacred oath! It's not a fucking game over here, you know!' Disgusted, she threw her arms up in the air. 'Just fuck off and go home.'

For some minutes they sat in the silence of the forest. Neither of them knew what to do or say next; all possibilities seemed wrong. Finally, it was Maria, by nature quick to flare but equally swift to gain equilibrium, who gathered her thoughts.

'Thomas. I have real feelings for you. I know how I feel. Even if you don't. If your marriage is a good one, then I don't want to wreck it. I'm only asking — not to pry, it's just … I have to know.'

Tom didn't have a throwaway one-liner about love. For the early years of his adult life he had waited to be hit between the eyes with it, but it never appeared. At first he'd thought the right person hadn't come along. Later, he reasoned that perhaps *he* was at fault, that there was something lacking in him to provide the fertile ground necessary for such a love to take hold. As for feelings, he barely knew about those either. He supposed they must be there somewhere, but if they did exist then they were buried beneath a quagmire of emotional gristle.

'Sometimes I look at you Thomas, and it's as if you are half dead. And then something happens, and you ignite and become more fully alive than the living, as if you are making up for lost time.'

He had no answer to her observation, though it certainly struck a chord. She turned to him and reached out to brush him on the cheek. 'What is it you're after?'

Tom slid onto his back. The earth cooled his overheated body. He looked at the trunk of a tree in front of him and followed it from its roots to the heavens, hoping that its course might provide an answer.

'Maria,' he said, 'since I've been in the Philippines questions have come to me. Big questions for the first time since my childhood. There is something here, in this country ... a spirit demanding engagement. So I have been trying, do you see? Though perhaps I'm even less sure about things than I was before.'

'What are you fearful of?'

'I don't know. Does it have to be fear? Maybe, deep down, there's vulnerability. I've been having the weirdest dreams, remembering things long buried. Sometimes I'll be walking across a park near my home, or swimming in the sea, and then I get this strange feeling that I'm emerging from a dream. It's happened all my life, as long as I can remember. I don't know what it is.'

Maria turned her gaze towards the forest. He tried to embrace her but she dodged his grasp, jumped up and moved further into the trees. She skipped and danced past fern-covered stumps and sidestepped rocks. He chased her, but with each step his heavy frame fell further behind. He tried jumping across a small ravine to cut her off, but as he was about to grab her he stubbed his toe on a tree root.

He fell, contorted in pain, only for her jeers to greet him. 'Oh, Thomas. You are such a big man. Such a wonderful hunter. But what a surprise you cannot even catch a *girl*!'

He pretended to be far more hurt than he was. He lay there silently and after a time she became worried and ventured close. In an instant he turned, jumped up and darted at her, tackling her to the ground. At first she resisted, trying to break from his hold. But this resistance proved fleeting.

They embraced with force — as if to brand imprints of their bodies onto each other's flesh forever.

* * *

They came for them in the hour before dawn. The first thing Tom felt was a shattering kick to the ribs. He awoke and stared up at a figure dressed in a military uniform. The man was shouting at him and it took some time to register what was happening. Tom reached for his clothes, but then remembered he had left them on the edge of the clearing. The man yelled at Maria and when she shouted back he kicked her hard in the back, grabbed a fistful of hair and swung her to her feet.

Tom stood to intervene, only to receive a blow with the butt of the soldier's rifle. It glanced off the side of his head, making him stagger. He felt the wound, immediately wet and warm with blood, as the soldier kicked him along the ground towards the clearing, holding Maria in an arm lock as she screamed at them in Filipino and English.

Before they reached the village, the familiar humming noise began to resonate across the mountain. At first it was barely perceptible, but soon it took on the timbre of a deep growl, and then finally an all-consuming beating drum.

Tom connected the sound to his earlier excursion to the rebel troops near Bampakan. The forest's canopy shook violently. The force of it stripped leaves from their moorings, sent entire branches crashing to the forest floor, and set off a chorus of animals and birds screaming in cacophonous terror. After the noise and the wind came the light. The helicopter searchlights probed the darkness. Flares turned night into an orange-filtered day.

Their captor finally managed to get them to the clearing where the village lay. Tom saw soldiers abseiling from the choppers, and others coming into the glade along the land bridge. In the stark light, he saw the soldiers enter the huts and drag their occupants outside, some naked, some in night clothes. He caught a glimpse of Paul, naked from the waist down, dressed only in his Mickey Mouse t-shirt. A soldier, toting a machine gun in his right hand, had him by the back of the neck, shoving him towards a huddle of men. Tom tried shouting out to him but to no avail, his words swallowed by the violent noise.

But it was the look on the villagers' faces that broke Tom's heart: utter dismay. To witness the children's fright and bewilderment was almost too much to take. They had been plucked from their slumber, the safety of their beds, their hearths. Even the warriors looked defenceless, their oaths of death and glory caught napping.

After some time, some sort of pattern emerged from the initial mayhem. The soldiers pushed Tom and Maria, along with the tribe, towards a field away from their dwellings. Men, women and children knotted together, at first mute, and then the crying and whimpering began as mothers tried to soothe their children.

As soon as they were dumped on the ground, Maria investigated Tom's head wound, growing pale when she realised its extent: the left-hand side of his face a watershed of bloody rivulets. She stood and began to speak calmly to one of the soldiers. At first he gestured for her to sit back down but she brandished her press credentials, showed the soldier the extent of Tom's wound and demanded to speak to his superior. Even as a captive she held her head high.

Within minutes, the soldier escorted her away. She returned a short while later, fully dressed, with a bandage and some of Tom's clothes bundled in her arms. She helped him dress and then bathed his wound with water the soldiers had permitted her to gather from the nearby stream. She bandaged him tightly, wrapping from under his chin over the crown of his head.

Tom felt a queer absence of pain, though he did notice that his body was shivering a little, his head numb, pins and needles running up and down his neck.

He also felt no fear. Removed. A passive object in his own story. What unravelled before his eyes took on the appearance of a dream world, as if holographic images were beaming up against the backdrop of the trees and the night sky. He noticed that some of the soldiers did not wear the uniforms of the regular Army. Some were Westerners. One soldier, with red hair and a moustache, looked vaguely familiar. Tom thought he looked Australian. He tried to place him but couldn't. He tried to yell out but his voice slurred and caught in his throat.

Tom was vaguely aware of the chattering villagers around him, questioning each other about what might happen next. But the period for anticipation was brief. Without warning, the soldiers started to set the huts alight, one by one. The smoke and flames quickly engulfed the buildings. Tips of liquid blue licked the edges of the forest, moist leaves hissed into nothingness. As each hut went up, the cries of the B'laan intensified until a wall of wailing, a high pitch of anguish, rose up.

When the blaze was at its peak, the soldiers began to slaughter the buffalos and the goats, slashing their jugular veins with knives and machetes. From where Tom stood, he watched as they dragged one poor beast and pushed it down the village well, deliberately polluting the water source. Bellowing desperately, it struggled to climb out. But soon the water turned crimson, splashing up over the side of the well, and the animal's head lolled to one side, sinking beneath the surface. The rest of the animals moved about their yard in agitation. With their throats cut, the flow of the herd's communal blood increased and, one by one, they dropped to their knees, stunned. Tom thought there was something noble about their faces as their lives drained away, the waning of their lives ending with silent dignity. Finally they dropped completely to the ground, convulsing amidst a sea of black mud blended with a royal purple gore, drowning in their own fluids.

Still, it was not over. The soldiers assembled the villagers again and moved them to the entrance of the clearing next to the land bridge, separating the men from the women and children. Then the soldiers set alight the field the villagers had so recently occupied. Annual crops, fruit trees, the animals: all gone in the inferno. There was nothing left but the stench of burning flesh.

Eventually, the invaders separated Maria and Tom, even though Maria thrust her press card into their faces. Then she did it once too often, and the redheaded soldier struck her down with a punch to her stomach. Tom, shocked from his torpor, instinctively stood to offer some resistance, but he too took another blow, this time across his back. He bent down low over Maria as she lay on the ground, deeply winded, labouring for a breath big enough to nourish her. But even as she struggled, two Filipino soldiers dragged her away towards the other women.

The military now gathered the men — including Tom and Paul — into two files, beginning their quick march down the mountain. Helicopters rose from the earth and fanned the flames now engulfing the field. As Tom and the other men moved across the land bridge, the cries of the women and children started to sink into his core, their laments burning into his bones.

10

The Truth

Not one arrow had been released, not one spear thrown at the aggressors. The women and children were now hopelessly exposed, Tom thought, and the men feared the worst. He sensed a feeling of shame among the men. He stumbled along with the rest of them, the pain so intense he felt no tiredness in his legs, incapable of comprehending what had happened a couple of hours before. He was beyond caring; his fate rested in the hands of others.

Full daylight emerged just after they reached the plain beneath the mountain. The sun, wreathed in smoke, created shades of gold and ochre more reminiscent of sunset than sunrise. It was not only the men who were silent and withdrawn. Dawn's creatures had fled to their nests, their burrows. The whole mountain and its surrounds were mute.

On reaching flatter ground, the men were loaded onto four troop transports. Paul and Tom were split and Tom dropped asleep many times, but these naps only lasted seconds. Each jolt of the truck jerked him back to a sudden and aching consciousness. In moments of lucidity, he became aware of the men around him, huddled together as infants nestle into their mothers. There was no sign of the chief. *God knows what's happened to him*, Tom thought. But Timon sat in the far corner, his face averted from the others, his nakedness in stark contrast to the grandness of the battledress he'd previously worn with such pride. This man's home had been reduced to ash, his family broken, his land seized.

Through the opening in the canvas at the back of the truck, he watched their convoy move through villages and small towns, the people busily going about their daily tasks, oblivious to the fate of those who passed before them. For much of the day, Tom felt sentient enough to understand that the number of towns they were passing through was decreasing, and that they were moving away from civilisation rather than towards it. From noon onwards, the forest's canopy grew thick again, with the convoy toiling over an interminable succession of mountain ranges, Tom's ears popping constantly with the changes of altitude.

Late in the afternoon, as the trucks laboured up the leeward side of one of the peaks, it suddenly grew cold. Most of the men were not fully dressed and, for the remaining hours leading up to dusk, the chill added to their horror.

When at last the convoy came to a halt, Tom saw the high concrete walls topped with barbed wire. Soldiers ordered the men to get out of the trucks. When Timon wouldn't disembark, a huge prison guard with tattoos etched across the bridge of his nose entered the vehicle. Tom heard Timon gasp as the guard kicked him with heavy boots. Dragging the young man by the hair to the edge of the truck's tray, the guard kicked him again, until the chief's son finally fell to the ground, his body inert in the mud.

Guards took most of the men through a maze of narrow, dim corridors to their cells. There were no beds in the cells, though each prisoner had a blanket to wrap himself in, providing some respite from the concrete floor. An open sewer flowed one way and then the other through the base of one wall. But most of the time the sewerage just sat there, rising with an invisible tide, occasionally flooding its banks.

There was no window and no ventilation in the cells. The stench had bones. Reinforced steel protruded from the walls where concrete had been roughly bagged on, as if construction had never really been finished.

For the rest of the first day and evening, the guards left their captives to their own devices. A small pot of rice and a tin bucket of water had been pushed into the cells, but they received no official visitors, nor interrogators.

To his immense relief, Tom had been reunited with Paul when the guards pushed them into the cells, so as soon as the shock and concussion began to wear off he began attempting to piece together the situation.

'How long will they keep us?' he asked, knowing well enough that Paul had no answers.

'Who knows? Hopefully we'll find out soon.'

Paul's attacker had ripped handfuls of hair from his head. His t-shirt was crusted in dirt and blood, a foraged piece of cloth now thrown around his midriff.

'Where are we, do you think?' Tom asked.

'We travelled north. Somewhere in Northern Mindanao. Somewhere a long way from public view.'

'What's happened to Maria … the women?'

'God knows.'

'How long can the military hold us? Can we ask to see a lawyer? Or phone home? Do we get a phone call?'

'You've been watching too much American television. No. We won't get any phone calls. Nobody knows we're here. We'll remain here as long as the military wants us to remain.'

Silence fell again. Tom tried to push his brain into gear to make it work. 'Did you see those Westerners in strange uniforms when we were arrested? Who are they, do you reckon?'

'Don't know … yes, I did see them. About a half dozen or so. Probably mercenaries. Could be working for the Company, or could be part of the Army's anti-terrorist training force.'

Timon and one other warrior, Abu, also shared their cell. For the first forty-eight hours of his internment, Timon had wedged himself into a corner in the foetal position. He did not eat and he drank little. At times, he wept silently. Abu, an older man, sat over the chief's son, stroking his head, singing to him. On two or three occasions, Paul tried to intervene. He cupped his right hand, filled it with rice and tried to force Timon to eat, but with no success. At one stage Paul grew angry with Timon and dragged the blanket from beneath him in a bid to solicit from him some kind of rebuke, some response, but Timon stayed in a kind of self-induced coma.

On the third day the door opened with no warning, blinding the prisoners. Two prison guards threw buckets of water over them, hosed out floors and walls, unblocked the sewer and issued each man with a clean blanket. Still, Timon didn't move.

Tom felt a little better after the clean-up. The stench had lessened and the fresh blanket felt like the height of luxury.

'Paul, what about Timon? What is he suffering from, do you think? Can we get him a doctor?'

'Timon is dying. He is willing himself to death. He has taken the oath of *Dyandi*.' Paul looked directly at Tom and added, 'So now you know what it is to take this oath: "until the last drop of blood".' Paul buried his face in his hands.

Faced with this grave reminder, Tom began to wrestle with the facts. Instead of attempting to make sense of the past, he tried to think strategically. Somehow, he thought, they had to get the news of their capture out to the rest of the world, and he had to get medical treatment for Timon. *Get to a phone*, Tom thought. *Once people know the shocking truth, surely all will be put right*, he reasoned.

During the afternoon, he felt some renewed strength flow through his body. But Tom could sense the indignation bubbling within. There it was, he noticed, the same strength he had fed upon as a child.

He spent the remaining daylight hours in deep concentration, contemplating plans for their release and planning for a future campaign against the Company. Fury formed a block of uncontrolled power within him. To no-one in particular, he mumbled his increasingly frequent refrain, 'They don't know who they're messing with ... they've picked the wrong guy to fuck around with.' He decided to demand a hearing the next time the door opened.

But this type of strength ravaged his soul as well as his body, and the brief window of clarity that had opened for him slammed shut with disturbing ferocity. That evening he didn't feel hungry, and about an hour after nightfall he began to turn hot and cold. His body burned until the early hours of the morning, only to be replaced with a freezing chill before dawn. And then he couldn't get warm enough. He tried breathing under his blanket, but the concrete slab took his body warmth away like a thief.

By lunchtime of the fourth day, he couldn't move. His head felt like it had been placed in a vice, while the rest of his body ached, as if he'd been beaten up all over again. And then came the nausea and the diarrhoea. It seemed to Tom that his insides were becoming his outsides.

Still, at one stage he rallied, concentrating with all his might as he tried to move to the sewerage outlet, out of respect for his fellow inmates. But when he got to his feet, the messages from his brain to his legs were incoherent. He staggered and then fell against the opposite wall, his head crashing to the cement with a sickening thud.

In his unconsciousness, the house visited him again. In the dream, fierce, wet winds again battered its façade. Trees and shrubs jerked within the hand of the storm in spasms of terror. Tom approached from the front gate. He did not want to go in. But he had been here before. He must push into it. He must ignore his instinct to retreat.

Again, he pushed on through the derelict gate. And again, the bough from the tree crashed before him. Everything told him he was not wanted here. But this time he moved further inwards, seeking the source of dread.

Slowly, he moved through the ancient gardens, past daisy bushes with huge woody trunks and geraniums withered with age. He staggered upon a path slippery with moss and algae. Looking up, he noticed a single light bulb illuminating a room above the veranda in a sickly yellow. Tom walked towards the light. He mounted the veranda, then struggled to open the main door of the house. It gave at last. Mustiness and the old smell of fried food engulfed him. Internal walls were half covered with peeling wallpaper — the designs of a past era. Threadbare carpets revealed a tattered hessian base.

His confidence grew as he moved around the house, the sense of threat diminished. In fact, a strange familiarity washed over him. In one room, a couch was vaguely recognisable. In the kitchen, he was sure he'd seen that red and white-flecked laminated table before. But his newfound relief was short-lived. He came across another wing of the house, obscured during his earlier wanderings. This part of the house had fallen into a state of total disrepair. Dry rot had crawled up the walls and ivy pierced the putty membranes of door and window frames. At first, he was delighted that the house was larger than he originally supposed. *With some work it can be restored*, he thought.

He tried the handle to this additional door. It opened with a sudden wrench. It was full of furniture older than in the other rooms and he recoiled at the stench. Straight away, Tom sensed a force inside this new room. A palpable force. A force so powerful, so sinister, that Tom turned and ran from it, crashing into tables and chairs, tripping on dusty carpets, desperately searching for lost doorways. At last, gasping for air, he sprinted along the disused path, dodging debris, the night sky full of fire. The sea hissed and sighed on the shore below.

* * *

Tom felt Paul and Abu move him closer to the sewer. He knew they could do little else. A couple of times he heard Paul pounding on the door calling for help, but eventually his friend gave up. Paul dipped one of Tom's discarded socks into a bucket of water and used it to mop his brow. Tom tried to communicate with him, but no words could form on his lips.

'Be quiet, Tom. Rest. Save your strength. It will pass,' Paul said. 'Malaria always worsens before it gets better.'

Tom's plunge into illness seemed to snap Timon out of his private world of desolation, and in a sign of great benevolence he walked towards Tom and draped his precious blanket over him. But a thousand blankets could not stop the shivering. On the verge of unconsciousness yet again, Tom didn't want to be touched. He didn't even want to be noticed. He wanted to sink into the earth, to be taken away from his body. Yet he did not want to return to that house. There was nowhere to go. Instead, the concrete floor danced with him jowl to jowl. He thought of his family and considered his death. Tears formed with thoughts of his children without their father. He thought of his own father. He drifted into worlds that were unknown to him, universes of delirium, spectacularly vivid, yet indistinct.

There was something there … there in the caravan, between its plywood walls, that he did not want to remember. Don't stop now, he urged himself. At last he remembered the smell of his father, his beer breath encircling Tom from behind, pulling his pants down as he pretended to be asleep. His father's hand moved over Tom's mouth, muffling his child's confused cries of pain and betrayal. He swore Tom to silence, sobbing uncontrollably, 'Or the Devil will take us both.'

* * *

It was black when he awoke. Was this death? No. The cold press of the damp concrete beneath him and the stench of the cell reminded him that he was alive.

Someone was slapping him on the face. 'Thomas ... Thomas McMahon. Wake up. You must wake up now.'

It was a man's voice — familiar. Hands moved around the back of his body and hoisted him into a sitting position. A torch waved around somewhere in the passage outside the door and then he saw the profile of Father Ricardo doubled over him. The priest fed him mouthfuls of water. The priest was in the room with other men. *How can that be?* Tom thought. In the intermittent light he saw two men carrying Timon out; unconscious or dead, Tom couldn't make out.

'Quickly Thomas,' Father Ricardo was saying, 'If you can get to your feet, please do. We haven't a moment to lose.'

Tom tried to stand, but at the very moment he became upright he fell like a newborn foal. Ricardo whispered orders, stuck his head under one of Tom's arms while someone else held Tom up under the other. They shuffled out of the cell, quietly cursing as they crashed into the doorframe in the dark.

11

The Protest

He lay there motionless, staring up at the tin roof high above his little room, forgetting who he was. Tom had spent the last three days in bed, at the Catholic Community Hostel in Manila. In fact, it was the same bed he'd bunked down in on the first night he'd spent in the Philippines. On that first night he'd stuffed his tweed coat into the mattress to provide some relief from errant springs.

Now he had no coat; most of his clothes were gone. Some remained on the mountain after the violent departure, others had become so soiled by the filth of the prison cell they had become worthless, fit only for fire. He had even lost his brown shoes.

This morning, when he climbed into the shower cubicle at the end of the corridor, he hadn't been able to muster the effort to turn the nozzle off when he'd finished. Physically, he had the strength to do it but he couldn't see the point. He stood for almost an hour under the cascading water, fixing his eyes on one tile. In some ways, since coming to the Philippines, he felt as if he had been losing his essence. And now, after the prison, he felt overwhelmed by grief, a sense of crushing loss encircling him.

Finally, when his body was thoroughly waterlogged, he looked at his wrinkled hands and a voice inside his head asked, 'What would Tom McMahon do?' An answer came after some time: Tom would turn the water off, hop out of the shower and then go back to his room. He felt like he was becoming a third person to himself, a removed being living in a history book, his once-instinctive responses to life's patterns and events lost.

But in those three days he realised that amidst this wreckage there existed hope and a new type of strength. No longer did he feel the need to draw on the strength of repressed hatred. His wounds were now open to the air. Images brought on by delirium in the prison had remained with him, but now he had the will to confront his past head-on, to get on with his life.

During this time of convalescence, he drifted easily in and out of full consciousness. He often dreamt of the house. It was the same house he had confronted many times before: a front yard filled with the chaos and wreckage of past storms, ravaged by the will of the sea, paint peeling off in layers of blistered skin from the walls of the front porch. During these dreams, he often considered retreat. But he knew that to go back was to lose. He wanted to be whole again, to feel things, to love like others loved. He knew that to weaken in resolve now would be the end. One more time, he scratched for courage from the bottom of his well and swung back towards this house's front door with mock bravado, ready to face whatever confronted him.

In the first room there was nothing — only a coat rack standing by the wall. The floors had been stripped of their coverings, their edges stained with black boot polish. Newspaper clippings had been pasted onto the walls, their edges dog-eared and yellowing. There was a window in the room, but when he drew back the dust-ridden drapes they only revealed a brick wall.

There was another door. He swallowed the bile of true fear as it rose up into the back of his throat. Again he tried to open the door, but as he pushed it fell from its hinges, revealing a long passage. Ageing photos of people he couldn't name hung unevenly from a worn picture rail running the length of the narrow room. Men and women stared out in black and white eternity, rigid, in high collars and coats. When he came to another exit, he knew this was the last one. This was where the monster had retreated to.

He felt the force beyond the door, recognising its powerful malevolence at once. Exhausted, choked with terror but resolute, he pushed on and crossed this final threshold.

The pathetic creature was simpering by a stone hearth, cowering in its own excrement. Tom walked up to it, only a foot or so remaining between him and this object of terror. The smell, though rancid, seemed familiar. He looked into its bloodshot eyes and saw only fear. Any power it once possessed had gone. Tom felt his own hate for the creature depart from the door he had just come through, and in its place blew the first winds of mercy and forgiveness.

* * *

Father Ricardo was a constant visitor throughout this time, recounting for Tom's benefit their escape from the prison and departure from Mindanao by boat.

'I realised what had happened when I visited the village two days after the invasion by the military,' the priest explained. 'When I got there, the women and children — including Maria — were clustered together into two burnt-out huts, too terrified to venture outside in search of food or water. You and the men were incarcerated in Martinez Prison, an old Spanish gaol, refitted by the Americans during World War II, on the north of the island. It's used for the removal of indigenous peoples who *get in the way of progress* in Mindanao — as a place of final detention, I suppose.'

The priest then described the deal he'd struck with the military. No mention would be made in the media of the 'terrorist cleansing operation' on Mossy Mountain, or the arrest and imprisonment of Dr

McMahon. In exchange the authorities would release all of the men, including Timon and the chief, who had both survived the ordeal.

'But tell me more about Timon,' said Tom. Has his health picked up? Can he return to the village? He nearly died back there.'

'Yes, the shame that many of the men feel will have lasting effects. Some of the younger men have already moved away to General Santos City. We worry for them deeply; they have no money, no shelter. But Timon has his people's future on his shoulders. He is already arranging for them to return to Mossy Mountain, with the Church's help. Your presence might not have technically protected the villagers from these atrocities, but it's ended up saving most of their lives,' the priest said. Tom looked down at his hands.

'So now Thomas, you have experienced the sickness of poverty?' the priest exclaimed, sitting on the only other piece of furniture in the room, a wicker chair. A broad smile dominated his face.

'Yes, Father. I suppose you could say that,' Tom replied, nowhere near as cheerily.

'You've lost twenty pounds or so, I think. But it suits you. You were too big for the Philippines before,' said the priest. 'Now I am sure that you could run up a mountain! Today you are better, I believe.' This sounded less like an enquiry and more like an order. 'You will be ready to travel home this evening.'

Tom nodded.

'Good. But we have not finished with you yet, my friend! We have a very busy day planned for you.'

'But Father, I'd prefer to just take it a little easy.'

'Nonsense! You can take it easy, as you say, on the plane. It is a luxury to fly. Most people have to walk. Now ...' The priest pulled out a notepad. 'First, we have organised an interview for you on *Inside Philippines*. It is the main national morning news and current affairs program.'

'But Father — what can I say? Haven't we been gagged?'

'Just don't talk about the military. Don't talk about the prison. Maria Cortes tells me that the documents you managed to—'

'Maria is alright?' Tom asked the question he had been both dreading and avoiding.

'Yes. She is a soldier. She has seen it all before.'

'How did she get off the mountain?'

'She can tell you later. But now we must concentrate on the task at hand. The papers you *collected*, shall we say, at HMC headquarters will provide you with adequate material. Arguments about poor environmental management. You know, the stuff about marine disposal of their wastes, how it is illegal in your own country.'

'Father,' said Tom, 'you are against this type of argument. You've told me several times now.'

'Nonsense. It will do for now. It will provide the wedge. Now we must build criticism against the Company from Australia. It is the only argument your people will understand. They don't want to hear of our dispossession.'

But the priest's eyes were twinkling. Leaning forward, he touched Tom conspiratorially on the forearm and whispered, 'Don't tell anyone else, Dr McMahon, but you may have been right on this one minor point.' He coughed, consulted his notepad, then continued. 'After the interview, we will progress to a protest meeting outside the Australia-Philippines Chamber of Commerce. A conference run by the Australian mining industry is being held there. You will present the conference chair with a report from our International Fact-Finding Mission demanding that HMC withdraws from its Mindanao operations directly. Of course, we will have media coverage. From there, you will go to the airport to catch your flight home to your loved ones.'

* * *

After breakfast, Paul drove both Ricardo and Tom directly to the studio in downtown Manila. Although Tom was still weak, the prospective media performance sent enough adrenaline through him to allow him to face the task. And the knowledge that, come what may, he'd be sitting on a 737 that evening gave him a tremendous lift.

While Paul and Ricardo sat in the front of the van rapidly conversing in their own language, Tom jotted down some key points for the interview. He was an experienced media campaigner and the points were few and brief.

As the vehicle pulled up to the kerb his heart jumped at the sight of Maria nervously puffing on her cigarette, pacing in front of the main entrance. Although Tom noticed how thin and exhausted she looked from the trauma of the past week or so, he thought she still looked glorious.

It was the first time he had seen her in a dress. Its deep green folds fell about below her knees. He found the contrast between its richness of colour and her dark complexion striking. As he stepped from the car, Tom felt unsure how to greet her. He wanted to embrace her, to stroke her hair, to stare into her eyes. He wanted to ask her how she was, to ask what had happened after the men's departure from the mountain. But he wasn't sure about the status of their relationship, nor how to conduct it, in front of Father Ricardo.

His hesitation was short-lived. As soon as Maria saw the car, she walked up to all three men, briskly shook each of them by the hand and launched directly into their immediate business: 'You're late! Dr McMahon ... you're on air in five minutes.'

She pushed open the main door of the building, depositing Paul and the priest in the waiting room, leading Tom to the recording studio. Maria avoided eye contact with him as she asked, 'Have you prepared something to say?'

His heart banged against his ribs, feeling jittery in her presence. But he marshalled his nerves, his feelings for her, and listened intently to what she had to say. 'Yes. I've got a few points here,' he replied.

'Good. Here's the press release I have written. Emphasise just two points. First, argue that HMC is treating the indigenous people poorly, how this is a common form of behaviour for the Company. Next, use the line about them abusing the Philippines' environment. That's enough.'

Just before she ushered him into the studio she paused. 'I suppose Father Ricardo has explained not to mention what happened … you know, up there.' Her eyes flickered to his, but she swiftly averted her gaze away from him. With that, she pushed him through the door.

The interview began abruptly. There was no time for introductions. Lights flared and cameras pointed. Sitting opposite him, however, was the familiar face of HMC's public relations guru, Jenny Thompson. The interviewer, all teeth and American accent, began with, 'Dr McMahon, you have been part of a tour of Mindanao, looking at the operations of Horizon Mining Corporation, I have been told. Tell us, Dr McMahon, what has your Mission found?'

He began smoothly, his angle premeditated. 'HMC is like a hamburger chain. It follows its recipe book wherever it goes. Its product is always the same. It always uses the same ingredients. The most important ingredient, both in the Philippines and in Australia — and wherever it operates — is that it divides and rules the local indigenous peoples in a bid to confuse ancestral domain issues … in its efforts to ultimately disavow the people of their rights to their lands, and to control these lands for its own profit making.'

At this stage, Tom glanced up at Jenny Thompson, who appeared to him unflustered, her legs crossed in waxen glory. Taking a deep breath, he continued.

'The second most important ingredient is that it operates in a manner which pursues the cheapest environmental management options it can get away with. In Australia, it has a very poor record in environmental management but here, in the Philippines, its record is even worse. In my hands I have an unreleased report produced by the Company, which explains that it will be using the marine disposal method for waste generated at its newly proposed mine at Bampakan.'

'Please explain the marine disposal method,' requested the presenter.

'Well, it is a method that is illegal in Australia and most other First World economies. Its environmental impacts are just too devastating. Basically, after the most cursory primary treatment, the toxic wastes are dumped directly into the sea. In the case of Mindanao, this would decimate river systems, as well as the fishing industries which support the coastal communities.'

'If I may say something on this subject, please David,' Jenny said. She didn't wait for the presenter's approval. 'I'm afraid Dr McMahon has misinterpreted an interim report prepared by one of our consultants. Horizon Mining Corporation has an international reputation as one of the leading proponents of best practice management in the environmental field. In fact, only last month it won an international award from the Worldwide Fund for the Environment for its efforts in this area.'

'Yes, but are these claims of marine disposal correct?' asked the interviewer.

'This is just one of the methods being reviewed by HMC. The Filipino people can rest assured that, in conjunction with their government, we will do the best thing for them and for their environment. By looking after the environment, we are conscious that we are looking after our business. Business is good for the environment and the environment is good for business.'

Tom was not sure how long he could watch her spin the sustainable-use dogma, straight out of the manual.

'Excuse me, David,' he said. 'But the crucial issue for me is that marine disposal would never be considered in Australia. It is illegal. Its environmental impacts are immense. In the Philippines, HMC are pursuing it because they can get away with it. It's cheaper.'

'I'd like to remind Dr McMahon that HMC rigidly adheres to the laws of the country it operates within,' Jenny said.

'It writes the laws,' Tom retorted.

The presenter, sensing a loss of control, was quick to seize back the initiative. 'Dr McMahon. It is true, isn't it, that companies like HMC bring opportunities for progress to areas of the Philippines that are underdeveloped.'

'Indeed, it's true David. But this development is short-term, while its social and environmental devastation is long-term. Anyway, most of the money made through these developments does not go to the people themselves but goes directly offshore.'

At this point, Jenny Thompson started to lose some of her sheen. It seemed to Tom she was growing more agitated.

'David, you must understand that Dr McMahon and his environmentalist organisation in Australia do not represent the majority of Australians,' she said. 'They stir trouble up in their own country, and now they are making it over here. He has a reputation in Australia as a radical and a critic. He is critical of everything, whereas HMC is a builder. It is easy to be critical, to be a *talker*. We are more interested in being *doers*.'

At the end of the interview, after the microphones were off but before the heat of the lights had dissipated, a shaken Thompson moved over to him. 'Dr McMahon,' she said, 'I just want you to know you've gone too far over here. You've made enemies, powerful enemies. And not just in the mining industry. You've alienated your own Environment Centre as well. I know ... I've been talking with your staff. Your own university, also, is distancing itself from your activities. If you want to fight with the big boys — well, consider the fight on. But I wouldn't like to be in your shoes.'

Tom was quite surprised by her outburst. He had expected more control, and was pleased with the fact that he'd obviously pushed the right buttons.

'Jenny, you don't know the half of it. While you're smarming yourself all over the local media, people are actually dying. Go back and tell the cowards who are your employers that they don't have a chance.'

Maria, who had entered the studio once the recording session was over, broke up the conversation. 'You really came over well, Thomas. Really well.'

Jenny Thompson, pretending to be oblivious to Maria's existence, gathered up her belongings.

'She is a bitch, that one,' spat Maria, loud enough for the other woman to hear as she left.

But Tom had moved past the interview. He was far more interested in Maria. Now liberated from the gaze of the priest he said, 'Maria. It's wonderful to see you. Are you alright?'

He moved to kiss her on the cheek, but she backed away.

'Yes, I'm alright.'

'I'm sorry I had to leave you on the mountain. But ... you know I had no choice.'

'I don't blame you, Thomas. I'm fine now. It's not for you to worry.'

'You know that I have to leave today, straight after the rally.'

'Yes, I know. Paul told me.'

She moved to the door of the studio, intimating that the conversation was over.

But he took her by the hand. 'Maria, are you angry with me?'

'I am not angry with you. It's over, that's all. Just something that happened on the mountain. You'll go home today, go back to your nice life, with your nice wife and nice children.'

'Maria. You're being unfair.'

'Unfair? Fucking *unfair*? What's that supposed to mean? You told me once that the Philippines made you feel certain things … things you haven't felt for a long time. Well, I'm just part of the broader experience for you, aren't I? You're over here on some kind of heroic mission. Trying to help us. The great white hunter! But really, you're as bad as HMC. Only, they're mining the earth and you're mining whatever.' Maria fidgeted with her cigarette lighter and then added, 'No … that's it — you're mining emotions.'

He was completely taken aback. He was already grieving at her loss, of not being able to hold her once again. But worse, he knew there were ribbons of truth in what she'd said.

'My feelings for you are real, Maria. You should hear yourself. This is coming from someone who's accused me — many times — of too much intellectualising!'

'That may be. But get this through your thick skull, Thomas. Only the people can save themselves. It's time for you to go home and deal with your own people.'

With that, Tom lost hold of her hand as she turned to the door. Before leaving the room she faced him once more, the corners of her mouth twisted up, and said, 'And Thomas, one more thing. You told me on the mountain … the Philippines forced you to confront your past. But it seems to me … you're just as terrified about your future. Perhaps one day I'll visit you there. Only this time, I might play the tourist. How would you like that?'

Before Tom could answer, she pushed through the studio door, ending the conversation.

As he followed her down the passage, they came across Father Ricardo and Paul in the waiting room, positively beaming.

'Thomas McMahon, you should have been in the movies,' the priest exclaimed. 'A majestic performance! And you were so polite!'

'Yes, bravo my friend,' Paul said, pulling Tom towards him in a hug.

'But quickly, we shall be late for the protest,' Ricardo said. 'Paul, bring the van to the front of the building.'

* * *

A mass of people — some five hundred or so — gathered outside the Hotel Paradiso inside the bustling district of the stock exchange. Within its lavish glass and marble façade lay the venue for the symposium held by the Australian mining industry. There was no way into the hotel, which was blockaded by at least two hundred men in assorted uniforms. Some wore the livery of the police, others the military. The majority wore unmarked white coats over black pants.

When Tom asked the priest who they were, Father Ricardo told him they were security forces. The police and military bore machine guns and other automatic weapons, their belts stuffed with grenades and ammunition. The white-coats were more understated, carrying pistols and revolvers.

At the entrance to the hotel car park, the battleline had been drawn. A jeepney, with the National People's Organisation's logo splashed over its side, perched on the footpath closest to the barrier of security personnel. Soon a large public announcement system was rigged up on its roof.

The first speaker was the protest organiser, a man referred to as Bong who Tom hadn't seen before. The crowd seemed to be growing. Most of them turned their heads in the direction of the loudspeakers on the vehicle, while others began to jostle the security guards on the barricade, flexing their collective muscle, measuring the force of the protestors' opposition.

Father Ricardo spoke next. Somehow, the priest had left Tom's side without him realising and now here he was standing on the jeepney's bonnet, wearing a red armband, with a fieldworker's bandana tied around his head.

'The B'laan people lead challenging yet simple lives,' Ricardo roared through the loudspeaker. 'They work hard and ask for little in return. They are not against mining. All they want is control over their own land, their own lives. When the time comes, it is up to the *people* to decide whether to mine or not. It is their decision — no-one else's!'

As he finished his short speech, he pumped a closed fist into the air for effect. *Definitely not like any priest I've ever seen*, Tom thought.

There was so much more Ricardo could have said: how the people had been harassed off their land; how the Company, through the medium of the military, had come in the night to inflict terror and devastation on the villagers opposing the mine. But the priest's sentiment was one that spoke of the humanity of the B'laan people. *Maybe that is enough*, Tom thought.

As the cavalcade of speakers continued, the language of an unreconstructed Marxism became increasingly apparent: 'imperialist plunder', 'global capitalism', 'the peasants versus the comprador class'. In Tom's country, such attacks on the power of capital had become subtler or even non-existent. But here, among the growing restlessness of the throng, the simple ideology of the battle between the haves and have-nots seemed totally alive.

Tom turned away from the speakers on the jeepney and surveyed the scene. He had been to many protests and organised several. He saw Paul on the other side of the cordon, talking calmly to the police.

Obviously Paul's job was to keep the lines of communication open with the police at all times. Protesting in Manila was a serious business, and although the crowd surged and convulsed as if in spontaneous raptures with the rhetoric of the speakers, most of the protesters were conscious of the clearly defined parameters that they moved within. Paul had to continually negotiate these parameters with police.

Beyond Paul were the huge doors of the Paradiso. The commotion at the front of the hotel had attracted some of its patrons. A line of Westerners shuffled down its steps, leaning back on the wall under the veranda.

Tom's initial suspicion that they were HMC delegates was confirmed at once when he spotted the very recognisable forms of Jenny Thompson and Roger Rumley, the head honcho of HMC, sauntering down the steps in an opulent charcoal suit. Tom remembered the last time he'd seen Rumley. The HMC boss had been out of his element that day in the grotty art-deco surrounds of the Environment Centre. Here, immersed in the marble and wood panelling of transnational hotel-land, he was well in his comfort zone.

After having spent a month with Filipino people, to Tom these Westerners looked odd to him. *Do they know of the atrocities, the level of dispossession, they are involved in?* Tom mused. Whether or not they were aware of their crimes, the suffering they inflicted was the same. He would fight them.

Scanning the entrance to the hotel, he saw Jenny Thompson talking behind her shoulder to someone in the foyer. He craned his neck to see. It was a woman … a blonde woman. *That looks like Louise*, Tom thought. Though he frantically tried to confirm his suspicion, the woman shifted back into the shadows of the foyer.

'Jesus Christ,' said Tom under his breath. 'Fucking Louise.'

He forced the issue to the back of his mind; the present demanded his full concentration. His name was being called over the loudspeakers. Paul grabbed him by the sleeve.

'Dr McMahon,' he said. 'We want you to address the rally.'

As he moved through the crowd, Father Ricardo saw him, clapped onto him and tied his red armband on him. 'Tell them, Thomas.'

Tom had no speech prepared, no dot points in mind. He stood gingerly at first on the bonnet of the jeepney, not knowing until the last second what words would come out of his mouth. He felt his throat tighten, sinews of angst jutting out from the side of his neck. He looked at the massive buildings, the towering skyscrapers of international traders recently constructed in Manila. Wispy clouds moved quickly across their turrets. He wanted to declare to the crowd, the world, just what had happened that night on Mossy Mountain, what had happened in that rancid hole they called a prison. But he could not for fear of harming the B'laan even more. His frustration burned in him, turning to fury.

His words formed. 'I come here today,' he began, emotion already cracking his voice, 'to apologise.'

The crowd hushed. Tom knew that most of them wouldn't understand what he was about to say. But, in many ways, he felt he was speaking *with* them, putting up all their hands to be counted before Rumley and his mining cronies.

'I want you to know that most of my countrymen and women have no idea of the crimes which are being committed against the Filipino people in the name of progress. I make no excuses for the actions of Horizon Mining Corporation. The Australian Government is complicit in the Company's operations in Mindanao. And the Australian Government is elected by the Australian people. We all know that ignorance is no excuse under any system of law. But most of my fellow citizens are ignorant to these acts, to these crimes.'

Tom pointed to the mining delegates, watching from the safety of the veranda. 'But there are some who are directly complicit in these crimes. I can see that some of the people from this mining symposium have come out from their five-star hotel. They appear to be quite amused by this gathering. Look, you can see them on the veranda — on the left there.'

The crowd must have been following the gist of what he'd been saying, because most of them turned to the people on the veranda. The smug countenance vanished on Rumley, Thompson and their cohorts; the blood conspicuously drained from their faces. No doubt, Tom imagined, that Louise was now cringing behind closed doors somewhere in the foyer, still out of view.

'What I say to you, Mr Rumley, Ms Thompson, is this: you cannot beat the people of Mindanao into submission. I have joined with them in taking a sacred oath. We have taken an oath to fight you to the last drop of blood. And fight we will.'

The rally began to roar in assent. Tom's raw emotion stirred them. He felt that he and the crowd were one. He pointed directly at Rumley and his colleagues. Now, shaking with rage and contempt, he continued.

'Yes, we will fight you. And I give the people here today my promise that although I will leave this country and return to my own — the country of HMC's head office — it is there that I will continue to fight. HMC, the people are against you ... and the people will win!'

The NPO activists in Manila hadn't seen him playing basketball with the youngsters back in General Santos City. They hadn't witnessed his attempts at hunting pigs. They couldn't imagine his body entwined with Maria's in the plantain field on Mossy Mountain. To them, he had been just another Westerner, a man of rationality and control. They had seen him only that morning on the television, when he had appeared balanced and reserved. They were unprepared for the force with which he addressed the crowd. If they had known of this character trait, they would never have asked him to speak. For this was not the time or place for revolution. This was a symbolic action designed for the media.

But now the crowd had turned towards the line.

Tom jumped down into them. Crowd-surfing on countless heads and hands, he somehow catapulted to the front. He saw Maria in the front line. She tried to push towards him through the seething mass. She was saying something he couldn't make out.

There was no time to savour endearments or imagined acts of contrition. He felt an energy snapping through the air and it was growing. It was the solidarity of the many and Tom could smell the honest indignation in it. He at once knew its properties.

The crowd moved forward towards the line, in concert, each participant's courage growing with the realisation that their body was now part of a larger animal, a creature of surprising vigour. The crowd had become a mob that wanted to spill the oppressor's blood in simple revenge. The mob's togetherness and its anger made the creature far stronger than its five hundred component parts.

Its first surge through the gate was effortless. The security forces, realising they had greatly underestimated the seriousness of the occasion, receded directly to the steps of the Hotel Paradiso. But their hasty withdrawal gave the mob room to gather pace. When the two lines collided, the people in the front ranks were sandwiched between the security forces and their own supporters.

Tom looked to his left and saw Maria next to him, buckling under the weight of the combined force, her back bent against its collective grain. *How did she get there?* he thought. He shoved the crook of his arm under her armpit and under that of an unknown man to his right. Bending his frame as far forward as he could, he pushed against the tide, all the time screaming at his newfound comrades in the front line, demanding that they link arms. For some moments no-one knew the outcome of this gigantic tug-of-war; then the crowd surged again, and the momentum was theirs.

The protestors now squeezed the security forces against the front of the building, trampling the rose gardens. Rumley had long since retreated into the foyer. Tom could see him clearly through the glass, his face marked with terror. Their eyes locked.

Just as the mob began to break the lines, to rush forward onto the veranda, the cracking of gunshots rang out. The mob, a creature for the first time sensing its own mortality, froze in its tracks. Tom was not sure of whether these shots had been volleyed into the crowd, or whether they were warning signals. Next came the tear gas. And then the water cannons started, somewhere from the right side of the building. The pressurised water hit them with such force that it pushed them onto their backs, taking both vision and sense of direction from them in an instant.

A hand grabbed the scruff of Tom's neck. Through the mayhem he saw that the hand was Paul's. Instinctively, Tom made a lurch for Maria, grabbing her arm. He would not leave her this time. Paul pushed and staggered his way through the bodies. Somehow he carved a path through the mass before them.

'Where is Father Ricardo?' yelled Tom. But Paul pushed on until they managed to leave the grounds of the hotel, people running everywhere, bouncing off everything and each other. He shoved Tom into a black sedan.

Paul shouted at the driver, 'Get him to the airport! Straight away!'

As the car sped off, Tom stared from the back window. Maria waved at him, ashen-faced, and then turned back towards the chaos.

12

Re-entry

Winter had come in his absence. An impenetrable greyness sat over everything, from the gothic stone of earlier Melbourne to the glass towers reflecting a sky without joy, reaching into clouds of smog and scudding out across Port Philip Bay. Even the organic world continued this theme of drabness, the power of the sun greatly diminished, its weakened light stark on the skeletal framework of deciduous trees now completely stripped of their leaves.

Tom checked the clock on the taxi's dashboard. It was peak hour in the afternoon, but the traffic seemed non-existent. He searched his mind for an answer as the cab left the airport freeway and entered the city proper. The footpaths, too, were strangely bare, devoid of people. And what few people he saw were huddled beneath high collars and coats, their faces sickly and desperate.

'Is it a public holiday or something?' he asked the driver.

'No, mate. Just a normal Thursday afternoon.'

He hadn't slept on the plane. For the first few hours, his mind and body had buzzed with random images from the protest. When he had quietened, he went straight to work, composing a press release on his laptop. He emailed it through to the Environment Centre as soon as the plane touched down, having marked it for immediate release.

An exhaustion he had not known in the Philippines now infused his whole being. Fish-eyed, he stared at familiar streets, their curbs and gutters absurdly clean. Thoughts of Amanda came and went, accompanied by an acrid and confused mixture of fondness and apprehension. He had not spoken to her on the phone since leaving General Santos City to return to Mossy Mountain over two weeks ago. Then came an apparition of Maria, like a kick in his belly. And then he remembered his children. Somewhere within him a spark of joy ignited, bringing an involuntary smile to his washed-out face. How he longed to hold them, to stroke their dear heads.

At last the taxi turned into his street, breaking his stream of contemplation. As he grabbed his bags from the boot, a hush swallowed him. Each rustle of his clothes, each crackle of his shoes on the curbside, were magnified. No birdcalls, no barking dogs, no people, no smell of burning leaves. As he opened the side gate and crunched down the path to the veranda, dread replaced hush.

With hands shaking, he unlocked the front door, calling down the passageway, 'I'm home!' But his vision of a delighted Emily trundling up the hall into his arms was not to be realised. Viewed from the central passageway, each room showed a bed made-up. The children's rooms, Tom thought, were too neat — absent of toys and other clutter. The mustiness of the house fanned his fears, and the note on the refrigerator confirmed them: 'Tom, we've left. I don't think you will be surprised. I know about your woman. Can contact the children through Mother. Amanda.'

'Fuck,' he muttered, snatching it off the fridge door, looking at it more intently this time. But the message stayed the same however many times he read it. How the hell could she know about Maria? He grabbed the telephone immediately and rang Amanda's mother, who lived in Canberra.

'Bernadette, it's Tom,' he said into the phone. 'I've just got back. Can I speak to Amanda … the children?'

'Tom … I was expecting your call. Don't panic. Of course you can speak to them. But they're not here.'

'Where are they?'

'Out. Look Tom, I expect you to be upset. But it's probably for the best for the moment … you've been gone without—'

'What do you mean it's for the best, Bernadette? Taking my children away from me without even a word, not even—'

'Tom, look who's calling the kettle black. You've been out of contact from your family, your work. Everyone's been trying to get a hold of you. And if what Amanda tells me is half true, then you haven't got a leg to stand on.'

He had always got on well with his mother-in-law. His indignation was short-lived as exhaustion seized him again. 'Bernadette, I'm sorry to go off at you. I'm just a bit tired … a bit shocked.'

'Don't be too shocked, Tom. From where I sit, it's been coming for some time. Who knows what the break might bring?' she added, hoping to end the conversation on a chirpier note.

'But the children. Can I speak to them?'

'I'll get Amanda to call as soon as they get home. Goodbye, Tom. Get some rest.'

Placing the receiver back down on its cradle, he remembered his bags were by the front door, still ajar. He couldn't summon the energy to bring them inside. Instead, he went back to the fridge and grabbed a beer. He drifted through the family room extension that both Amanda and he had been so proud of upon its first completion, out into the backyard. He slumped onto the lawn, though it was damp and cold.

The high fences surrounding the yard closed in on him like those of a familiar prison cell. And the all-too-recent malarial sweats revisited him now, not as severe as before, but febrile enough to make him strip off his coat, enough to cause nausea.

He stared at the fences — the private boundaries, the borders.

On the other side were people he barely knew by name. *There are no communities here*, Tom thought. *We are all completely isolated.*

He was snapped out of his reverie by the noise of high-heeled footsteps echoing down the hallway in the front of the house. His heart jolted with expectation — perhaps it was Amanda and the children.

He pushed himself up from the wet turf, all his energy and hopes restored in an instant. But this newfound strength left him as quickly as it came when he saw Louise, calling for him from the kitchen. She was dressed in a white suit; immaculate and cool, as always.

'Louise, what the hell are you doing here? How did you get in? How did you know I was back?'

'Oh, what sort of a greeting is that, Tom? The door was open. I tried knocking but there was no response.' She prowled around the kitchen like she owned it. She glanced at Amanda's goodbye note left on the kitchen bench, registering its key points, rapidly calculating possible scenarios. She opened the fridge. 'Mind if I help myself to a drink?'

Without waiting for a response, she found a bottle of Semillon, scrambled around for a glass and poured herself a generous portion. Tom sunk onto one of the stools by the breakfast bench, too deadened by fatigue and loss to object to anything she did. He just wanted her to leave so he could get some sleep.

She softened her voice, her stance. 'Poor dear, you must be exhausted.' Tom looked directly at her, his cold stare forcing her to avert her eyes. 'So where is the family?'

'Not here,' said Tom blankly.

'Listen, Tom. I know she's left you. Everyone knows.'

She selected a bottle of beer from the cooler and brought it around his side of the bench. She took the empty one out of his hand, and then thrust the fresh bottle back in its place. She turned a stool towards him, placing it against his and perched herself on it, invading his space without a second thought.

Gazing up at him, she began, 'Tom, the next little while could be tough for you.' Then taking a swig from her glass, she added, 'The Centre is not very happy with what's going on at the moment. They don't like being associated with this sort of *radicalism*. Your Dean — trying to "ascertain your whereabouts" as he called it — has also contacted us. For the last fortnight, I had no forwarding address. We were worried sick.'

'Alright Louise, who is *us*, who is the *we* you're talking about? Is it the Centre or is it HMC that you represent?'

'What the hell are you implying?'

'Louise, I saw you in Manila. I saw you at the Hotel Paradiso rubbing shoulders with Roger Rumley, Jenny Richards and the HMC crew.'

She must have been on the same plane back, Tom figured. Probably in business class. Hanging his head, he looked down at his hands and saw dirt from the Philippines still lodged under his nails.

'That day at the Centre. When we met with Rumley and the rest ... about the bullshit magazine, about their bullshit consultative committee. You just couldn't accept saying no to the Company, could you?'

For a few short moments, Louise did her best to look aghast. Then, realising that her cover had been blown, she changed tack. She stomped to the sink and threw half a glass of wine down the drain.

'We know everything about what's been going on, Tom. You want to talk bullshit? I'll give you bullshit ... all this crap about saving the poor Filipinos from the big mining villains! You were over there getting your rocks off with some of the local talent — that's what all our reports tell us!'

She reached for her matching white bag and pulled a faxed piece of paper from it. Shoving it in front of him, she said sharply, 'Seen that before?'

He read the first sentence, recognising it instantly as the press release he drafted on the plane, the one he sent as soon as he had touched down.

'Do you think, in your right mind, that we are going to put the Environment Centre's name to that shit?'

'I'm the one who makes those decisions, Louise.'

'Not if the Council decides that you have over-stepped your mark.'

'There's nothing in that release that isn't verifiable fact, Louise. I've got the HMC report right here that backs it up, provides all the detail about their intentions to dump the mining waste straight into the sea.'

'So you say. I've already sent it to our lawyers for an opinion. I think you'll find it won't be released.'

She took the paper back and plunged it into her bag. Her coolness had returned. She gathered her possessions and made for the front of the house. Following her to the door, Tom felt the first sensations of relief, knowing that it was nearly over. She swivelled on the veranda. Tom hung back in the doorway.

'By the way Tom, your distinction between the Environment Centre and HMC is an outdated one. You have been away for a long time, haven't you?'

Tom looked perplexed.

'HMC has applied for full membership of the Environment Centre.'

He laughed out loud. 'Oh yeah — on what grounds?'

'On the grounds that they are a sustainable developer, a major sponsor in our climate change campaign.'

'Over my dead body.'

'If you look at the constitution, Dr McMahon, you'll notice that sustainable development is our primary objective, not insurrection in the forests of Mindanao.'

* * *

That night, at the border crossing between sleep and wakefulness, the telephone rang from the hall. It was Amanda. On first hearing her voice, a feeling of loss seized Tom, tears welling in his eyes.

'Amanda, it's so wonderful to hear your voice … I thought you'd never ring.'

'Well, there's been a lot to sort out,' Amanda said, distant and cautious.

'I'm not complaining, Amanda. I'm the one in the wrong. I just really miss you. I miss the children. I feel like I'm walking around with no arms. Can I speak to them?' He began to sob, trying to finish his sentence between gasps of air.

Amanda had only heard him cry twice before. At the birth of both their children. It caught her unawares, softening her.

'Never mind, Tom. Look, you can't speak to them now, they're asleep.'

'Are they all right? I mean, how are they? Are they okay?'

'They're fine, Tom. They're well, and they miss you too. We're flying down next week. You'll see them then. We'll be staying at my sister's.' Then she added, 'Well, I better let you get some sleep. I expect you've got a big day tomorrow.'

Tom was touched by her solicitude, even if unintended. It reminded him of days gone by, days which seemed far away now, when they shared this very bed he was lying in.

'Amanda,' he said, searching for the right words, 'I'm really sorry for what's happened. I blame myself. I don't know what to do at the moment, whether to fight for you or let you go.'

'Tom, we let each other go a long time ago.'

He knew she was right. One thing had become glaringly clear. It was his children that he had to fight for now.

'Could you do me a favour?' he said, choking up again when he realised the seriousness of what she had just said.

'Depends what it is.'

'Could you tell the children I love them — that I'll love them forever.'

'They already know that, Tom.'

'Yes, but could you still tell them … from me?' he persisted.

There was a pause on the end of the phone. Tom thought he could hear Amanda crying, but he couldn't be certain. He was overcome with such a grief that his ears were ringing, his vision blurred. At last her voice came back along the line. 'Of course I'll tell them.'

* * *

For the entire first week of Tom's return, each new day had started early; he was still on Philippines time. On the sixth day, at about five-thirty, an hour before winter's dawn, he heard the newsagent's van rattle down his street. He reached for his robe, shoved on his slippers and walked out the front door.

The wind off the sea had momentarily ceased its onslaught, with a drizzle of water falling straight down from the blackened sky. Tom breathed in the bitter smells and tastes of smouldering wood and sappy resins. Seeping from the chimney stacks of shutdown combustion stoves, the fumes mixed with the damp atmosphere to form a noxious brew.

Cursing, he searched for a good thirty seconds before he found the plastic-wrapped newspaper — in a different hiding place each morning, this time lodged between the brush fence and the wet foliage of the plumbago hedge. Jumping back under the cover of the veranda, he pulled the paper out of its sleeve.

Careful to close the front door behind him, he shuffled back down the hallway — still shrouded in night — blindly turning over the front pages of *The National.* Switching the lights on in the kitchen, he filled and turned the kettle on, spread the paper out on the kitchen bench and anxiously began flicking through it.

After going through it a third time he finally accepted that his story wasn't there, that it hadn't been there all week, and it was never going to be there. Since his return, leading up to this moment, Tom had deliberately decided to avoid the Environment Centre. But now, with the successful blocking of his press release, Louise had forced his hand. With a renewed sense of urgency, he rang for a cab that delivered him to the Centre by eight in the morning.

By ten o'clock, he had sorted through a mound of his neglected correspondence and already it was clear that Louise had been prolific in her casting of vitriol against him in his absence. The Centre's lawyers, on Louise's advice, had indeed stymied his press release, and she had quashed his usual opinion piece in *Green Options.* Worse still, many of the old die-hards with whom he had developed trusting relationships over the years were unwilling to return his calls.

His relationship with the university's administration had also taken a frosty turn. He'd managed to antagonise his Dean, the Chancellor and the Vice-Chancellor and consequently an official investigation was underway regarding his actions. Tom realised that he didn't care.

He was finding it almost impossible to get his story out in Australia. The voice of Father Ricardo rang in his ears. In one of their many conversations on Mindanao, Tom had claimed that in Australia 'at least you weren't shot for what you said'.

'In Australia, you can't say anything worth getting shot for,' the priest had replied.

It wasn't so much that the press was controlled by the few and the powerful. In Tom's case, the censorship occurred before the press even received the information.

There were two happy pieces of correspondence in the pile. One was a postcard from Patrick Walters. The photo on the front showed some sort of rodent, fossicking around bushland. Scrawled on the back were the words: 'You shoved it up the stick-nest rat! Good on ya! Patrick.' Tom laughed out loud. *Bloody Patrick*, he thought, smiling to himself.

And then there was a letter from his friend Paul. Apparently, Tom's testimony on television and in other parts of the press in the Philippines had gone down well. Whether it was the quality and weight of his evidence, or whether the time for the issue had just come, the case against HMC had moved out of the political periphery previously dominated by the National People's Organisation. The matter was no longer a radical issue but was now firmly in the mainstream. According to Paul, largely on the testimony gathered by the International Fact-Finding Mission and the publicity that followed it, the Catholic Church had redoubled its efforts to close down HMC's exploration phase on Mossy Mountain, before the Company progressed any further.

While still digesting the contents of the letter, on the spur of the moment Tom rang his friend in Manila. He felt kind of surprised when Paul answered, thinking the connections between the two worlds more fragile, more uncertain.

'Paul, it's Tom. Tom McMahon.'

'I can hardly mistake that accent!' Paul answered excitedly. 'How are you?!'

'Pretty good, my friend. I just got your letter and couldn't resist ringing you.'

'You just got it?'

'Haven't been in the office. You didn't mention Timon and the chief... the villagers? Are they alright? Father Ricardo mentioned to me last time that not all the men returned.'

'The chief's very being has been diminished; it's hard to describe. Timon's alright. He's actually very strong. He's taken over from his father now.'

'Please remember me to him, Paul.'

'I will do. Yes, most of them moved back to Mossy Mountain. It's funny, after the trashing of the village, it's the women who've taken more of a lead on the issues. You know, organising and making decisions. They've even started up a collective educating other villages under threat in western Mindanao. Some of them have travelled up to Manila with Maria to take on the government face to face.'

'Maria?' responded Tom, the breath momentarily taken from him.

'Yes, she's been unstoppable. A real driving force.' Paul paused and Tom sensed there were other things his friend wanted to say. But after a few seconds of silence, Paul continued on a different tack. 'But look, I wrote that letter a week ago. Have you heard the latest?'

'Just what you wrote me.'

'It gets even better! The Global Bank has withdrawn its funding and support! But it is even better than that … HMC is pulling out of Mindanao! Look, let me see if I've got the press release … here it is. I'll read it for you. It's brief but to the point: "Today, Horizon Mining Corporation has opted to withdraw from its mining operations in Mindanao, citing problems with the quality of the ore base and political instability in the region as its major reasons for doing so."'

The two men talked excitedly for over an hour. They dissected the campaign against the Company, discussing the possible next moves by HMC who would, no doubt, re-emerge in Mindanao under a different corporate guise. By the end, they had exhausted the issue entirely and the conversation turned to the personal.

'You know, I still think you were really stupid to take that vow up on the mountain.'

'I don't know, Paul. It seemed right at the time.'

'At least you've now been released from it. What will you do?'

Tom paused, collecting his thoughts. 'Things have changed at home. I think I've made another vow.'

'Not another one!' Paul laughed.

'Don't worry. This isn't me saving the world from evil oppressors or anything. It's just about getting closer to my kids. Being there for them.'

'Good on you, Thomas.'

'Keep in touch, Paul. Alright?'

'Will do, my friend.'

And as Tom hung up the phone, he muttered '*Dyandi*' under his breath, feeling the gift of this oath extend beyond the community he left behind, to his very own tribe at home.

* * *

The second week of his return, the children stayed with Tom all weekend. Emily and Jem spent most of their time playing in their rooms, relishing their old home, reacquainting themselves with the familiar. Most of the time, Tom sat with them quietly, joining in their games. Emily had practically brought her entire soft toy collection with her. She always played families with them, and he learned a lot of what was going on in her mind from participating. Tom thought she seemed, on the surface at least, comparatively untouched by the recent upheaval. Her dark ringlets bounced upon her shoulders, yelps of delight frequently interspersing her make-believe world.

It seemed to Tom that his son was more distant, more confused, more obviously hurt. For the first time, it worried Tom that Jem had his father's eyes; those of an adult's in an eight-year-old's skull. Already their bright lights of immeasurable hope, infinite possibilities, had dulled somewhat, now tarnished with his own early chapters of pain and bewilderment. As they kicked a footy to each other in the backyard, Tom noticed that Jem's body had lost its enthusiasm — the fearless commitment with which he had thrown himself at the ball in the past. He was more awkward, slightly disassociated. Tom decided to be direct with him.

'How's your new school, Jem?'

'Oh, alright,' he muttered sullenly.

'It's hard, isn't it? I remember changing schools when I was a kid. Making new friends and everything.'

The kicking and handballing continued for a while before Jem responded. At last he blurted out the question that went straight to the heart of the matter: 'Dad, what's happened between you and Mum?'

Tom dropped the ball, moved to his son and took his hands.

'Jem, I've got no simple answer for you. Sometimes married people grow apart.'

It was a line Tom had heard many times before. Now, to his disgust, he was using it himself.

'But what you must understand is that it's got nothing to do with you. It's about Mummy and me.' Tom swallowed hard before progressing. 'Jem, there's only one thing you really need to know. I love you, will always look after you, will always be your father. Nothing can ever change that.'

The dam broke. Jem burst into tears, huddling within his father's embrace.

Earlier that morning, while dropping off the kids, Amanda had briefly stayed for coffee. At first, she did not tackle anything that might have happened in the Philippines. She had concentrated on the here and now. After a while, once the children retreated to their rooms, she became more direct.

'But Tom — how can I say this in the nicest possible way? You look shocking! Your face is all drawn and haggard. And you look kind of ... yellow.'

'Oh, I'm alright. Lost a bit of weight over there. I'm coming good, though.' To Tom, Amanda still looked exquisite. Momentarily, he yearned for the familiarity of the past, to float in their sea of shared moments.

'You look beautiful, Amanda,' he had said, trying desperately to ignore his fear of rejection.

'Thanks, Tom,' she said, tears welling in her eyes. 'You haven't told me that in ... I don't know how long.'

He had moved to kiss her on the cheek, but she jerked back in alarm, nearly tumbling from her stool.

'No Tom, I'm sorry — not anymore. I'm certain there's no going back for us now, but I want the relationship to be a good one. For the children's sake. Besides ... I think I'm in love with Jack.'

In his heart of hearts, Tom really was expecting the first part of her response. But the last part came out of the blue.

'Jack Collins?' he had said. Jack's documentary had been the catalyst for sending him to the Philippines. He'd known him all his life.

'Yes ... Jack. He's been here for me. He knew what was going on in the Philippines. That helped a lot. And he happened to be in London when I was over for the conference. Besides, it seems you've got someone else.'

'I don't know what you've heard, or who has told you what. There was someone. But it's over.'

Tom thought Amanda seemed almost bored by this revelation. She appeared so much more advanced in the separation than he was. Of course, she had the benefit of more time. She also possessed the power and authority of the initiator, although Tom knew his behaviour over the past couple of years had contributed greatly to the current state of play. He recognised, again, his past fear, his cowardice — how he had never been able to instigate such a move of separation, how he had in some ways silently and unfairly cajoled his partner into making the first visible steps.

'Amanda … the children?' he said, eyes desperate. 'Are you all moving to Canberra to be with him?'

'We'll work something out,' she had said.

And Tom had said, 'As long as I can be near the kids.'

13

The Sea

Tom moved from the lounge room and the leaping fire of the cottage into what he had renamed the 'cloak room' — that purgatory between inside and outside. It was colder here — more vulnerable — in this nether land built of tin and ironbark, far removed from the squat safety of the cottage proper. Tom managed to free one hand to grab his wetsuit and flippers, and then battled with the back doorhandle using his knee and elbow.

At once the winter sea seized his eyes, forcing him to cast his gaze downwards. He heard the waves crash hard on the reef, no more than two hundred yards away. With shoulders set, Tom pushed forward. Wisps of salt water lashed his face and, rounding the shiny-leaf hedge, the wind blew him back a pace or two before he could adjust his lean and venture into the backyard. It was as close to a sea-going stance as one could adopt on land.

His backyard was an alien world in the late afternoon of winter. The first gum trees on this side of the Australian land mass were gripped in a stroke, their spines bent backwards, shrivelled canopies, feet fastened to the edge of this madness.

He passed more gums, overgrown gardens, the bulbous pepper tree that crouched over the shed. Through the back gate, Tom entered the moorland separating the house from the sea. As he moved across the dunes, away from the cottage, he heard the cries of his children from the backyard.

Tom had bought the children a kite, which Jem had mastered in minutes. Now he saw it climb high into the sky, then plunge towards the earth in downward spirals. Just before its inevitable collision with the earth — only metres from the ground — Jem jerked on the lines, righting it and sending it soaring gloriously back towards the heavens. Tom could see Emily waving at him, yelling something out to him, the wind catching and scattering her words.

Turning back towards the sea, a fresh, salty south-westerly immediately produced tears in his eyes as he ran over a carpet of seagrasses to the shifting mass of sand. Running along the dunes, he was the target of plovers, swooping, masquerading, lying about the proximity of their nests.

It was a purple twilight when Tom arrived at the beach. He started out towards the black volcanic point. It was a place, Tom thought, where once a mountain had vomited its innards with such force that its stomach lining was blown here, hissing and cooling on its surprised meeting with the freezing waters of this ocean.

The entire front of his wetsuit was white with evening dew, the air delicious, the sand covered with the lightest layer of quicksilver. Each footprint made a hole in the moist layer, revealing light brown colours underneath. He bent down and picked up a mouthful of the ocean's soup and stuck it in his mouth, letting it trickle down into his beard. It was silent — this part of the beach utterly protected from the wind — apart from the crunch of his feet in the sand, huge clouds of steam coming from his mouth, and the cry of gulls.

Tom reflected upon the past months. His marriage had disintegrated and his previously rock solid moorings at the Environment Centre were now severed. Black squalls had overtaken his academic and activist lives, once the key and stable sources of his identity. He had lost his certitude, his confidence, and his signposts of meaning had shifted. He had stopped talking to his 'anonymous friend', but at the same time he knew his experience with the sacred was more alive than ever. And, alongside all of this, he also felt the first thrill of freedom, of self-determination.

With each new day, he saw things more clearly, experiencing emotions for which he did not yet have names. Threads of light presented themselves where before there had been a dank uniform blackness. Some weight, some impossible burden, had been lifted from his shoulders. He had nothing to fear. His senses were alive. The colours and possibilities of the world danced before him. Even the borders and boundaries of inanimate objects, such as a simple chair or kitchen table, seemed crisp, definitive, luminescent.

He began to discover certain things about himself, to learn about his wants and needs — the basics of life, those things he felt most people took for granted. He heard the voice of his heart, his instincts. And with these emotions came joy, and its bedfellow, pain.

It was a new kind of pain — not built from the stale bones of fear and hatred — but fresh, liquid and raw.

He decided that he had made the right decision in coming to Port Conway. For the first time in his life he felt truly at home — truly himself. From his new home by the sea, it was little more than an hour to Canberra, to the children. He had managed to get two days of casual teaching at a small college there. This had been a blessed relief. When he had resigned his university job in Melbourne, pre-empting the administration's final and determined moves against him, he'd been worried that he may never find employment in the tertiary sector again. The money was a pittance in comparison, but Tom didn't mind. He had enough to live on, plenty to provide support for Jem and Emily.

After moving to the Port, he'd thought of Maria many times. Visions of her came to him without warning. In his head, he had replayed the words of their last conversation over and over, and now they came to him again. He knew that she had been right. In some ways, he'd gone to the Philippines as an adventurer — however guileless — hiding behind the rhetoric of environment, liberation and solidarity, using the place and its people as a kind of spiritual playground. He now cringed at the thought of it.

But just when he'd dismissed his own good intentions, another part of him forced itself to be heard. 'But at least you befriended the suffering. The suffering need friends, remember? You honestly shared your life with them. And besides, wasn't it just the right thing to do?'

And then his body recalled another, different truth. He relived their passion, made greater by his fantasies. Slivers of time stolen from the mountain in Mindanao, past and imagined: Maria — slippery and shiny with sweat and ardour — pushing off the makeshift bed, pivoting on the balls of her feet until he felt he was going to expire with pleasure, that this ecstasy would take his last breath. He wanted to stroke her temples again, to kiss the saturated nape of her neck, to smooth out her sweat-congealed hair.

A bird lay on the edge of the shore. It had a fine, splayed black tale, webbed feet, a green down on the base of its neck, with the rest of its body shining white. Its neck lay back in complete repose. Its eyes were closed, utterly relaxed, with its head tucked back towards one side. Dew gathered around it, covering the sand. He could see that it was dry underneath and as soon as the dew fell on it, it seemed to disappear. *So the body must be warm*, he thought. Its soft beige chest and underbelly had feathers perfectly preened. But he could see no movement in its breast, no heartbeat. Gradually the dew began to settle on the body and around its closed eyes. It was then that he realised he had been there just after its moment of death. He imagined an exhausted bird struggling to find land in this wind. It had aimed at the red beacon of Warden Head lighthouse and, upon reaching land, had fallen in exhaustion on the first piece of shore.

Tom suddenly possessed a strange desire to touch its breast, to feel whether it was warm or if it just looked that way. But part of him was irked at touching this peculiar creature from the sky and the sea in its early moments of death. So he pushed on up the beach, head down, into the wind. No more than one hundred metres up the beach, he turned around. *I have to touch it,* he decided.

He stared at the bird from above, the sea now lapping at its feet. He bent down, timidly touching its downy underbelly. It was warm. With more confidence now, he stroked it affectionately. He smiled to himself, thinking that not long ago he would have been too afraid to touch it. And there was more: Tom imagined something of its life pass through to him, something of the sky and the sea. The beauty of it, he thought, this extraordinary foreign creature asleep permanently on the sand, by the sea. He considered burying it, throwing some sand over its body, to protect its eyes briefly from the sharp beaks of the gulls. Then he reasoned: this being from the sky has no place in the ground.

It should lie in the open.

Tom turned to the ocean now and spilt his lungs into the barrels of the sea. Screaming with all the strength of his soul, he emptied his hurt onto the vastness. Nature's Confessional. Now, strangely elated, he moved out onto the black reef.

About the author

Timothy Doyle is Professor of Politics and International Studies in the School of History and Politics at the University of Adelaide in Australia; and Chair of Politics and International Relations in SPIRE at Keele University, United Kingdom. He has been a dedicated environmental and human rights activist since the 1980s. He is currently serving as Chair of the Indo-Pacific Governance Research Centre; and Director of Human and Environmental Security for the Indian Ocean Research Group. He lives in Adelaide, Australia; and Staffordshire, in the UK.

www.ingramcontent.com/pod-product-compliance
Lightning Source LLC
Chambersburg PA
CBHW071435260626
47170CB00008B/2725